JANE FEAVER

Love Me Tender

VINTAGE BOOKS
London

Published by Vintage 2010

2 4 6 8 10 9 7 5 3 1

Copyright © Jane Feaver 2009

Jane Feaver has asserted her right under the Copyright, Designs and
Patents Act 1988 to be identified as the author of this work

First published in Great Britain in 2009 by
Harvill Secker

Vintage
Random House, 20 Vauxhall Bridge Road,
London SW1V 2SA

www.vintage-books.co.uk

Addresses for companies within The Random House Group Limited
can be found at: www.randomhouse.co.uk/offices.htm

The Random House Group Limited Reg. No. 954009

A CIP catalogue record for this book
is available from the British Library

ISBN 9780099521280

The Random House Group Limited supports The Forest
Stewardship Council (FSC), the leading international forest
certification organisation. All our titles that are printed on
Greenpeace approved FSC certified paper carry the FSC logo.
Our paper procurement policy can be found at:
www.rbooks.co.uk/environment

Printed and bound in Great Britain by
CPI Bookmarque, Croydon CR0 4TD

for Matt and Esther

If anything can, even by only the remotest chance, operate as a trap, some animal will end up trapped in it.

Ted Hughes, *Moortown Diary*

CONTENTS

THE MAYOR OF BUCKLEIGH

The car was full of shopping and Lauren was squashed in the back. Casey – although he was only seven – had got the passenger seat. He was eating Hula Hoops, holding them provocatively above his head so she could see. Lauren was kicking the back of his seat. Debbie, their mother, was on automatic. They were driving home through the lanes the back way. Leaves from the hedgerows were mulched in the road, heaped like clothes. Debbie had slowed to take a sharp bend when, without warning, a huge vehicle appeared to leap into the lane ahead of them.

For a moment she lost her bearings. She thumped the brake, twisting the steering wheel blindly towards the hedge. The car came to a stop with a thud and the three of them jolted forward. Still heading straight for them, the broad silver grille of a Land Rover – the belting embrace as the two cars met.

The silence that followed was like snow. Then the Land Rover started up and pulled back, came to a standstill a few feet off, chugging over. A door opened and a leg appeared; a tall man with thin, floppy hair climbed out. He came towards them with his hands on his hips, holding back the tartan lining of his jacket. He cast his eyes over the fronts of the two cars and rested his hand above Debbie's door, peering in under the arch of his arm.

'No real damage,' he said casually. 'You all right?'

'You were coming way too fast,' Debbie said, clutching the steering wheel.

'Long as no one's hurt, that's the main thing.'

He lowered his head further, searching out Lauren in the back. He had watery eyes set deep in their sockets. She could smell dog on him.

'Lanes are slippy, this weather. Not much you can do –'

Debbie ignored him, turning to Casey.

'You all right?'

Casey was scrunching the metallic crisp packet. He shrank down into his seat and tossed it over his shoulder into the back.

'Lauren?' she said, looking up, seeking her daughter's reflection in the mirror.

Lauren didn't want to make a fuss. She nodded.

Not prepared to concede ground, Debbie said, 'Bloody lucky.'

'As I said. Knock for Knock. No damage to speak of.'

Debbie was tired, she wanted to get home. She shook the gearstick. If she'd been a man she might have got out and squared up to him. It went against her sense of justice to let it go. But she was tired.

Lauren was watching him and wondering if he was nice or not. He was dressed like a teacher. Maybe the crash might be a good thing in disguise.

The man gave the car a pat. 'Well, then,' he said and combed back his flop of hair, stalking back to his own car.

Debbie shook herself, started the engine, put the gearstick into reverse and pulled back into the verge to let him pass.

'Tosser,' she said under her breath.

When they got back to the bungalow she went straight round to inspect the front of the car. The headlight was smashed, trailing a wire. There was steam from the socket and grey plastic stretched like chewing gum when she poked the glass. The side of the bonnet was buckled.

'Lying git,' she said, and then, furious as she continued to prod at the car, 'No damage! Bastard.'

'Dad'd learn him,' Casey said coolly. 'He'd smash his face in.'

'We're not telling your dad.'

'Why?'

'Because.'

'Why?'

'Because I say so – shut it, Casey, that's enough.'

Debbie knelt by the wing, as if by looking long enough the damage would mend. Lauren stood behind her. 'Is it broken, Mum?'

Debbie snapped at her. 'You've got eyes. Of course it's bloody broken.' Casey sneered at Lauren and flicked his fingers gleefully.

'Shithead,' she said. Under a microscope the hair on his scalp would resemble a doll's, each hole, a sprout of hair. He had a raspberry rash at the back which he kept scratching until there were scabs. And he smelt of cheese; he never cleaned his teeth.

'Need a hammer?' Casey asked.

On Monday, before school, Debbie took the car up the road to the garage at the edge of town. She pulled up, out of the way of the petrol pumps, and made the kids wait for her in the back seat. The door to the shopfront bleeped when she went in. There were big windows with Christmas lights already – red and green – flashing. Lauren could see the colours splashing her mother's pale jacket as she sat down by the desk to wait. There was a ripple in the glass. A door had opened, someone walked in.

It was a tall man wearing a dark boiler suit, skinny and bald. He was a bit lopsided and leaned to wipe his hand on his side as he came towards her. She raised herself a little from the chair, and then her head began to bop about, talking; at one point she twisted round to point out the car. He had a long chin which he lifted to follow her gaze. Then he stood behind the desk and leaned over to write something down. Lauren watched her mother joggling in her handbag, handing him keys. When she stood up and came out of the door, she turned back to say, 'Thanks again.' She had a skip in her step.

'No worries,' the man replied, raising his hand and lowering his head shyly.

Debbie was breathless as she opened the car door for them. 'Come on. Out. We'll walk from here. He's going to sort the car for us. Hurry up, it's not far – you'll be late.'

The air smelt of seaside and coal. Lauren pulled her sleeves down to cover her fingers. Casey had already begun to wander off into the cave beside the shop where a van was raised up on stilts. A short old man with a missing tooth came out to head him off, a spanner in his hand.

'Casey!' Debbie called to him, exasperated. Casey never did what he was told.

'Don't mind him,' the man said, lifting his hand to his forehead. 'You new?'

'-ish,' Debbie said. 'Couple of months we've been here now.'

'Pleased to meet you. Stan,' he said, holding out his hand and indicating up to the sign the length of the building. '*Simmonds* – Stan, that's me. And Barry – you've just met him – that's the "son".'

He didn't tell them then that Barry was the mayor. And they didn't find out, not until he started coming round for his tea and watching telly with them, sitting on the settee with Debbie.

Lauren hated the countryside. It was too dark. In London, the lights were always on and everywhere glinted; here it was pitch black. Debbie had said, though she and their dad were getting divorced, it wouldn't make much difference; or where they lived: they'd see him as much as they ever did. Down here, she said, they'd have a better life – wait and see.

Their dad was in the desert now, and in the second bedroom in the bungalow, with the duvet over her head,

Lauren tried to imagine she was in a tent flapping its canvas. The harrumphing outside was camels, just like the model he'd brought back for her last time, real camel skin – its eyes two black beads – which she kept on a shelf by her bed.

The morning after the first night Barry stayed at Debbie's, the wheelie bins from the top of the high street were discovered lurched on to their sides helter-skelter down the hill. Somehow Barry felt implicated in their abandon; he was assiduously putting them straight, lifting them with as little noise as possible in his progress from the bungalow to the house.

When he got back, Stan was already out of bed. He didn't say a word, sitting at the kitchen table drinking noisily, the blue mug of tea rising and falling. Everything he might have said – *your mother, your mother, your mother* – flooded round the room.

All day long at work Barry thought of Debbie, the press of her skin. That evening, he couldn't sleep. He'd never been with anyone like her – a woman with kids in tow who talked sometimes as if she were a man. It wouldn't have been possible when his mother was alive.

The wind was worse than ever, like blankets in his ears. In the middle of the night he woke in a sweat, as if there was something personal in it: the violence had the force of a fist. Debbie was from London. The only time he'd ever been there was on a school trip. What he'd remembered was not the dinosaurs or the buttons in the Science Museum, but the force of a Tube train approaching through a tunnel – the terror of being pushed or jostled by the crush of bodies on the platform.

He couldn't stop thinking about her: the way she'd sit next to him on the sofa, with the kids sprawled on the floor watching TV, and her hand would be in his trousers, holding on to him with a private smile on her face. The kids would occasionally look round and he would feel as if she'd got a gun to his head, so wound up he could cry. He'd have to go out the back before tea, adjust himself, breathe in the creosote and felting of the roof. But he'd never shake off the dull primed sense of anticipation, tense in every muscle like a trap had been set, its springs bursting to snap on a soft rabbit neck.

'Fuck off!' the boy had said to his sister. That kid, Casey, a piece of work. He needed a good slap.

'Listen to him,' Debbie called out from the kitchen, as if it were something to be proud of. 'Casey – that's enough.'

He picked it up from school, she said. Nothing she could do. But the delivery, Barry thought, where'd he get that from? The way his eyes narrowed to slits.

The kids took ages to go to bed. Casey'd be in and out like a ferret. They'd end up with hardly any time to themselves, sitting on the sofa, her with her knees up, him tapping an empty can of beer.

'You never married?' she asked.

He paused. 'I was, once.'

She shifted round. 'Were you?'

'Didn't work out.'

'Divorced?'

He nodded.

'Where's she now?'

'Torquay – she was last time I knew, anyway.'

'Kids?'

'No. Thankfully.'

'You don't want kids?'

'Not bothered . . . to be honest.'

She took the can from him and put it down on the coffee table. The wind was thudding down the chimney, making the flames in the gas fire gutter and hiss. There was a smile about her lips when she said, 'Save you going home in this.'

He felt silly saying he needed an early night. 'Must be my age,' he said.

'Bet you're not as past it as you think –'

The sheets made the hairs on his legs crackle; they were a peachy colour, with tiny balls of grey fluff where they were turned over. He kept his pants on. She appeared in the doorway in a man's shirt and slippers.

'Does it make me Mayoress?' she laughed, making her way to the end of the bed, diving towards him, wriggling up alongside his waist. 'Do you ever wear your necklace in bed?'

'It's a chain,' he corrected half-heartedly, intensely aware of the warmth of her hand fumbling for him. 'Your "chain of honour",' – she said as his stomach caved in – 'Your John Travolta.'

Her breasts, when she drew back the curtains of the shirt, astonished him. They felt like suede, and they hung, slightly different in weight, two soft birds, each with its blister of an eye.

She had chiselled herself underneath him and he propped himself on his elbow, not to squash her. She was helping him at first, guiding him in. But then she seemed to retreat, lying inert, watching him as if from the bank of a river, as he was bowled away on a current too strong for him to help himself, whimpering cries as the water came up over his head and swallowed him whole.

Perhaps she betrayed the tiniest shudder – the involuntary shudder of an engine. He couldn't be sure. He twisted away, rubbed his face into the pillow.

She said nothing as they lay side by side and he began to worry that he'd been too quick. Then she huffed and raised herself, reached over for the box of tissues by the bed, pulled one out, and, practical, perfunctory, swabbed herself. She lay back motionless. Her eyes were looking straight into space, straight through the ceiling, through the roof.

The children were grumpy in the morning. It was half dark. 'There's sand in my eyes,' Lauren was complaining. Then: 'There's a girl in my class says her dad's sleeping in the shed.'

'Really?'

'They have rows. Her mum's got her a new phone. With a camera.'

'What's that got to do with it?'

Lauren shrugged.

Casey had a bowl in one hand and with the other was

holding up the trousers of his red pyjamas; he was shuffling towards the TV.

'Not in the lounge, Casey – in here! On a chair! You'll spill it.'

She'd given the children the last of the milk and blew over the bitter black coffee in her mug.

'Lauren, have any of your friends started their periods?'

Lauren glared at her and twisted in her chair to get down.

Casey began to snigger, spattering cornflakes across the table.

'I'm not talking to you, mister,' Debbie said. 'Block your ears.'

November was a month of storms. Bonfire Night was abandoned for the first time anyone could remember because of the evil combination of rain and high wind. By the time they arrived at the weekend of the carnival, things with Barry were a mess.

She'd become friendly with Trish, who took Casey and Lauren after school on the days Debbie worked. Trish was great with kids: the kids next door, the kids that she took charge of at youth club. Casey loved going round there: Trish's cupboards were full of snacks and she had a PlayStation permanently set up on the TV. Sometimes she'd sit down next to him when he played and every time he punched the air, she'd punch it too.

Trish was fat and she had the baby face that went with being overweight. Recently little things about her had begun to irritate Debbie. Increasingly, every time Trish said something about Lauren or Casey, she would take it as a criticism.

'Do it for the kids,' Trish had said, 'they love dressing up for Carnival.'

Sitting getting ready for the parade in Trish's front lounge, Lauren was already on the verge of tears. At the last minute Casey had refused to dress up, and so the full weight of responsibility for not letting down the little girls next door had fallen on her.

As Trish worked on the girls, Debbie dealt with Lauren. But she was jumpy, keeping an eye out through the mesh curtains for the band, whom she could see beginning to congregate in their purple jackets.

Lauren was dressed in one of Casey's vests. Her hair was pulled up under a school swimming cap that Debbie was daubing with the same yellow paint she'd used on her arms and her face.

'Loser,' Casey mouthed to her.

Trish had spent weeks perfecting Marge and Lisa costumes, watching episodes of *The Simpsons* and making sketches. She had sculpted two headdresses – a tower of purple and a yellow hedgehog – from offcuts of industrial foam. These were now lowered ceremonially on to the blonde heads of the girls, who were arrayed in tunics that had been constructed painstakingly – a long-standing Buckleigh tradition – from a thousand tiny twists of jewel-coloured crêpe paper. It was clear that Lauren's costume, which had been left to Debbie, had been put together at the last minute.

Debbie was smarting from the insinuation that she didn't think about her kids.

'It's different in the country,' Trish had said. 'You have to be careful. People notice. Tongues wag.'

Trish had been encouraging about Barry – they'd had a laugh together over it – but when it came to Robert Woodward, she'd gone cold. Robert was first euphonium in the band and worked on the meat counter in Somerfield. He'd offered Debbie a piece of sausage on a cocktail stick, right into her mouth.

Barry was nice, but he didn't particularly set her world alight. Mr Woodward had been into the primary school with some of the younger members of the band to drum up new recruits, and Casey had been sent home with a cornet and a number to ring if she wanted him to have lessons. For the first time she could remember, Casey was keen. It would be good for him, she'd thought, give him something to do.

'Brrr.' Trish sounded like a horse, as they trailed at the tag end of the procession. Then she said brightly, 'Hope Barry's not going to hold it against the kids?'

Debbie bristled. 'What do you mean?'

'He's the mayor. He'll be judging – hope he'll give them a fair crack.'

'Why shouldn't he?'

'Who's to say? Sour grapes?'

Debbie'd caught sight of Robert, who was a big man. He was warming up the mouthpiece of his instrument. Now the sight of his lips made her feel sick – the way he'd pulled at her breast, his spongy fingers reaching up her skirt for the elastic of her knickers, spreading her out on the settee, saying how he liked to give individual lessons.

The procession turned off into the marketplace and pulled up in front of the main showpiece: a trailer, done out in white and mauve for the Carnival Queen. Trish was at Debbie's elbow, pointing out Wendy Fuller, the builder's daughter, the way she must have been stitched into the material of her mauve and silver dress; how the hem had been Wonder-Webbed and not sewn, trailing where she'd caught her heel in it. Wendy was liver-lipped. Although it was freezing, there were dark purple patches of sweat in the fabric under her arms. She had a tiny page and a bridesmaid who sat at her feet on white crêpe-covered boxes, shivering without complaint, seeing this as one of life's inexplicable obligations like drinking milk, or learning to sit cross-legged in assembly.

The presentation was from the chairman of the borough council, Mr Percival. Barry, as Mayor, was at his side, tactfully at one remove while the ladies briefed him, hastily giving the cup a last polish on their sleeves. Mr Percival took to the mobile steps of the trailer, his hand on the knot of his tie.

In the love-heart line of her dress, Wendy's breasts were dimpled and large as two ostrich eggs. Mr Percival, almost down on one knee, handed her the cup. 'My great pleasure,' he said, looking round to his audience, 'to present to a young lady – absolutely gorgeous, if I might say – this—'

'Hold on, do that again, please, guvnor,' said the man from the *Courier*. 'The cup. Give it her again. Nice smile.'

Mr Percival winked at Wendy, holding his pose. 'Might have to get used to this: adoration, flash photography . . .'

Wendy clutched her trophy dumbly and Mr Percival was suddenly at a loss. There was a sense of anticlimax, people drifting off.

'Right. All done?' he said, rubbing his hands together briskly. The secretary of the Rotary Club motioned him down and he descended gratefully into her outstretched arms.

No one was paying further attention to the float, so when a commotion set up at the bottom of the steps – a sharp cry – it appeared to come from nowhere. And when people turned to look, they were amazed to see Mr Percival doubled up, cradling his stomach, struggling to contain himself because he was aware that he had a limited field from which to choose his words (children, ladies . . .).

Then there was another shriek, this time punctuated by the word 'Dickhead!' Debbie felt the blood drain from her face. She looked at Barry for the first time that day. The suit he was wearing was old-fashioned, double-breasted, made for a broader and shorter man than he was. She watched him lean forward, the chain hanging loose from his neck, and reach out for her son. But Casey, who was right in the middle of the fray, managed to dodge his grasp and hurled himself once again at Mr Percival's groin.

The secretary proffered her clipboard uselessly to the welter of flailing limbs and kicks that revolved like farm machinery.

There was a general rush to eschew responsibility. Trish was in Debbie's ear, saying, 'What on earth's got into him?'

Mr Percival was furiously dusting himself down. 'For heaven's sake!' he said, glowering at the boy who was standing in front of him, unrepentant.

'Pull yourself together,' Barry hissed, holding Casey at arm's length, looking straight across to Debbie as he said it.

She had no escape. 'Casey,' she called defiantly, as if she was calling off a dog.

'Wanker.'

'Casey!' Debbie grabbed him. 'Stop that, this second.' She could feel Barry's hot eyes on her and hear a group of old women tutting, raising eyebrows at one another. She dug her nails into her son, his bones so brittle they felt they might break under her fingers. She wanted walls of steel to come down and hive them off so she could lay into him and show him what it felt like to be so humiliated.

Casey was still muttering as if the words were being shaken out of him like coins. 'Stink bomb. Shithead.'

She couldn't bring herself to look at Barry, although she wanted to beseech him. *It isn't me. It isn't because of me.*

She hesitated as Mr Percival continued to bat at his legs, straightening his cuffs and his tie. She couldn't help thinking that there was something familiar about him – perhaps no more than anger, or disdain. She said to Casey, for the benefit of onlookers, 'It's Lauren's day! Why do you have to ruin it?' Then she turned him away from the knot of people, one arm bent behind his back. 'You – pig!'

17

She marched him over to the Market Hall where the judging was going to take place for the different categories of fancy dress. As they went they were pelted by a sudden confetti of hail. People began running inside to take cover. Through the doors the hall opened up wide as a hangar, pigeons walking high-wire along the steel rafters.

'Sit down.' She threw Casey towards the far end of a long trestle table where Lauren was waiting with Trish and the two girls. Trish was making final adjustments to hair. The girls were sitting patiently in a row with their hands pressed under their thighs.

'Sit,' Debbie hissed at Casey, raising her eyes at Trish. 'Not a word!'

Casey sprawled.

Debbie turned her back on the others and said to him, 'Why do you do this to me?' She was like a terrier, shaking, and she wouldn't let it go. 'I've a good mind to ring your dad. Go and live with him – he'd not put up with it.'

Casey stared at the ground and then said in a take-it-or-leave-it voice, 'It was him. The man in the car.'

'What d'you mean?' she said, but letting it dawn on her, a picture respooling in her mind of the dark slicked head coming out of the Land Rover, the long limbs, the greasy skin.

'I don't care,' she said, floundering. 'I don't bloody care. You've made a worse show of me – worse than him.' She didn't want to be reminded of the car. She'd let the whole incident go. Nothing had been said, but Barry had sorted it and never asked her for any money, and, as long as she didn't have to think about it, that was fine with her.

'How long have we got to hang around in here?' she snapped. 'Why can't they get on with it?'

A few days later the winds broke all records. A tornado was registered fifteen miles to the west, ripping its way through a farmyard, upending a chicken coop, taking the corrugated roof off a barn.

'You'd never think we were in England,' Debbie said, convinced their own roof would fly off. The thundering in the flue was so loud they couldn't hear the TV.

Lauren said, 'It's like a tent.'

'No,' Debbie said, doubtfully, 'it's stronger than a tent. We'll be OK.' But the living-room door kept blowing open.

'Shut it on your way out,' she said to Casey for what felt like the hundredth time, packing him off finally to his bedroom.

Not long after, there was a rapping at the front of the house. Debbie went to look. A shot of cold air whistled through the letter box and she could see the dark imprint of someone in the frosted glass. She squeezed past the two bikes in the hallway and unlocked the door. It was Barry standing there, his face blown about, holding a box of Celebrations.

'What's this for?' she said. 'Come in.'

'I won't stay. It's just . . . I didn't want you to think – the Fancy Dress – not my decision. It's the WI decides. I just get to read them out.'

Lauren was making a stable for her ponies under a chair. She was embarrassed to be caught playing with them and

19

positioned herself with her back to the chair legs in an attempt to hide them from him.

'Like a drink?' Debbie asked.

Barry made a bid to look at his watch. The numbers danced.

'A beer?' she urged.

'Thanks.'

'No hard feelings?'

'Not at all,' Debbie said.

Casey was in the bedroom playing through the ringtones on Debbie's mobile. Lauren willed him to stay there, not to spoil things.

Her mother went through to the kitchen, the kiss of the fridge, the hiss of a can opening.

Barry looked down at his hands, where the dirt was ingrained like a tattoo. He glanced at Lauren and tried to find some resemblance to her mother. Lauren was darker, more delicate-looking.

'Like your slippers,' he said. She was wearing her tiger ones.

'How's school?' he asked.

'OK,' she said.

Lauren hated school. They'd stopped sending her home when she complained of stomach cramps because it was becoming a habit. At breaktimes they let her sit in the library. It was growing pains, they said.

'Did you like school?' she asked shyly.

'Who does?' he said, giving a snort. 'Show me someone who does.'

It comforted her, talking to him. He acted as if he was interested.

'What've you got there?' he said, bending forward to look under the chair.

'Nothing.'

'Horses?'

She realised then that she didn't think of them as horses. They had names. She played with them as if they were people.

Debbie came back into the room with a can in each hand. 'Not showing him your ponies, are you?'

Lauren could feel the sides of her neck burning; she moved backwards, sitting on a hoof that pressed like a hard pea into her thigh.

'Cheers!'

As if in response there was a blast from the bedroom, an elephantine creature clearing its throat.

'Not now!' Debbie yelled, and a shot of beer flew up like foam through a bore hole. The noise erupted again, three wobbly notes descending.

'He's taken it up, then?' Barry said.

'It won't last,' Debbie said. 'Nothing does.'

'What about you?' He said, 'Didn't you fancy it?'

'Haven't got the puff.' Debbie glanced at him suspiciously, wondering if he was making a dig.

'I hate it,' said Lauren. 'It sounds like farting.'

'Lauren!' Debbie looked again at Barry, with the can at her mouth until the metal began to stick to her lips. She turned to Lauren.

'Bed.'

Once Lauren would have made a fuss about being the oldest and being allowed to stay up later, but she got up without a murmur.

'Make sure Casey does his teeth for me, takes his clothes off?'

'Night night,' Barry said, and then when she'd left the room, 'She's a good girl.'

'She has her moments,' Debbie acknowledged.

'She's a credit to you.'

Debbie looked up at him. He was sitting earnestly with his hands knotted in his lap. She softened – an unfamiliar sensation of warmth and gratitude towards him. She was kneeling on the carpet parallel to his legs and leaned in very slightly, plaiting a strip of green pony mane between her fingers. It was hard on your own. Really hard.

Barry didn't stay that night and at the time, Debbie thought he'd never come back.

When he'd gone she opened the bottle of Bailey's she'd bought for Christmas and drank half of it down. In the middle of the night Casey had blundered into her bed, wet the bed, so that at one o'clock she was wandering round the bungalow with sheets trailing from her arms like a ghost.

She took him in with her. He was only a little boy, she thought, tucking him up in a towel; but all the trouble of a man. It seemed incredibly quiet now as she lay holding him. As if it had been him all along, like the wind –

22

raging about the place. She pulled the covers up over his shoulders. She loved him like that, his little breaths, his open puffy lips, wiped of all intent, as if butter wouldn't melt.

GREG AND SARAH

Growing up, Greg thought that Sarah hated him. She used to say he stank, that his friends were nerds. 'Gross,' she'd say when he lay on his bed naked, steaming from his bath, 'you freak.' Since she'd gone to college, they'd had little to do with one another; nowadays she didn't come home more than a couple of times a year.

There were no guests this Christmas apart from Gran, their mother's mother. They'd just finished lunch. Bill, their dad, was concentrating hard, squirming in his seat. He cleared his throat.

'Going to find something softer to sit on,' he said, excusing himself, wiping his mouth with a holly napkin.

'Right, Mother,' he said, making an effort to raise his voice, using the table to hoist himself to his feet. 'Going to join me?'

Gran was partially deaf with eyes like frosted glass. She farted as she let Bill guide her by the elbow through to the living room.

Sarah rolled her eyes and slumped forward on to the place mat of yellow roses. She made a noise into the crook of her arm like a bee trying to get out of a window.

* * *

Last year, things had been different. Greg had Claire with him; he got to sit with her on the settee, his arm around her.

'No one told me she would be here,' Sarah'd protested to their mother in the kitchen. 'You could have said something.'

'What difference does it make?' Jean said, shaking her off. 'You're here now. Don't make a fuss.'

'Tell him to stop smooching then, in front of everyone.'

'She's a nice girl.'

Jean was fussing more than usual to find a double set of knives and forks for the table; she brought out a new pack of napkins. This was the first girl Greg had brought home.

'My girlfriend,' he'd started to say.

Jean had been unbearably attentive, exclaiming when Claire offered to help with the washing-up, giving her a tour of the cutlery drawers, the cupboards where she kept her mixing bowls and pans.

It was clear that she approved of the girl: the sleek line of her hair, the neat, clacky heels, her tiny rabbit-bone ankles. Claire too went out of her way to please, extolling the Methodists who ran the youth club, the dances they used to perform as little girls in flame-coloured leotards.

'She's a lovely smile,' their mother said, full of hope, over the phone to a friend.

It was the sort of smile you learned from looking at magazines: a neat segment like a piece of orange.

*   *   *

'Do you like my titties?' Claire had asked Greg when they were on their own, turning towards him and offering them to him in the cups of her hands. She had the biggest boobs he'd ever seen and all he wanted to do was touch. But, pounding with desire, he was aware of movement around the small house. He knew someone would be bound to catch them.

Everything else about Claire was tiny. In her clothes the labels read 'petite' or XS. It made Greg think of her as a doll. When she sat on his knee, her hair against his chin was soft as fur; it smelt of cake.

'You take Claire up, will you?' their mother had said to Sarah. 'Show her where she's sleeping?'

Claire had been given Sarah's bed – floral sheets put on specially – and Sarah was going to have to sleep downstairs on the couch.

Sarah came back so infrequently that her bedroom had been taken over by Jean's knitting machine, her childhood bed moved into her brother's larger room, where it was used as an extension to his wardrobe. Jean had made Greg clear the bed for Christmas and, after a brief moral debate with herself, she'd put Claire up there with him. In this, she wasn't exactly encouraging nocturnal activity – they were twins after all – but hoping proximity might help cement her son's relationship.

'*His* girlfriend,' Sarah said. 'Why can't he do it? He's got bloody legs.'

Sarah used to swear in front of her mother just to wind her up.

The first thing Claire said to Greg when she'd followed him up the stairs and he'd pointed out where she'd be sleeping – parallel to him in the twin bed – was, 'I don't think your sister likes me.' She sat down on the end of the bed and gave a little bounce.

'Who cares?' Greg said, kneeling down at her feet, taking the hem of her skirt between his fingers, 'I do.'

A whole year had passed since then. After lunch, when Dad had taken Gran off to Uncle Mick's, Greg had gone upstairs. Sarah was left with Jean, who was upset, clattering dishes to little obvious effect.

'He doesn't have a clue how to look after her. He won't have changed the sheets since last year.' Jean had buried her hands in a lava of water. Mick was her brother and she'd fallen out with him several years ago over foot and mouth. He'd given up on farming, selling off the livestock, letting out the land from the farm that had been in the family for generations. He was intent now on converting the barns into holiday lets. Jean couldn't bear to be in the same room as him. At Christmases, they'd agreed to ferry Gran between them.

'Is that it?' Sarah asked.

'You can go,' her mother sighed, as if she were on her hands and knees. But before Sarah could escape, she added pointedly, 'Incidentally, you can always take them back if you don't like them.'

Sarah began to fold the tea towel, half on half, and then again, until it was a small square in her hands.

'*Marks* are good about giving your money back. You could swap them.'

'They're fine.'

'I wasn't sure if they were your sort of thing – I never know nowadays.'

Her mother was like a goat at a fence. Sarah had already buried the knickers at the bottom of her case. Ten pairs of sturdy, pink, thermal shorts.

She said, deliberately cool, 'It won't change who I am, you know – if that's what you mean.'

Jean blenched, shaking her hands over the sink, feeling her skin tingling as if it would dissolve. 'Do you think I'm stupid?' she said in her quavery voice. 'You think I'm so ignorant, don't you, Miss high-and-mighty.'

'Oh God. Will you leave the knickers out of it?'

'I can only try, you know. I try my best to understand.'

'Can we leave it for today, please?'

Greg was lying flat on his back, cupping a hand over the zip of his jeans, watching a fat winter fly work its way around a brown spot on the ceiling. He'd eaten too much, and was now burping Brussels sprouts and bitter tinned chestnuts. His gums were jangling – he worried constantly about his teeth. He was thinking in circles, the minute repetitions of a fly's manoeuvrings: how last Christmas it had all been ahead of him, creeping upstairs that night after everyone else, pulling the bedroom door softly to, crouching in here, where Claire had been lying, in his new pyjamas. He'd been nervous, reaching his hand under the quilt and stroking

31

what he decided must have been her knee. Her eyes were closed but, without a murmur, she reached down and moved his hand up against her nylon knickers so that he could feel the scratchy press of her like a swallow's nest. He'd kept completely still, as if his hand had been glued to her.

When Sarah put her head around the door, the fly dropped and began buzzing angrily in a clot of dust. The room stank of his aftershave. She sat down on the mattress and the headboard rocked against the wall.

'Feel,' she said after a while, hoiking up her sleeve and making a fist. 'Pure muscle, that. You should try it – a good workout – it'd take your mind off things.'

It was no surprise to Greg that Claire and Sarah hadn't got on. They had nothing in common. Sarah scoffed at make-up. Claire told him that his sister was stuck-up. Just because she'd been to college didn't make her any better – and the way she read the newspaper, showing off.

Greg had resolved not to tell her anything; he didn't want to give her the satisfaction or the ammunition. Sarah continued to hold her arm under his nose until, grudgingly, he touched the skin there. It was taut but soft, pliable as plasticine. The smell was plasticine too. He was tempted to say he wouldn't want a girl he was going out with to look like that. But instead he made a shrug of approval.

Sarah had been pretty as a child, with thick, white-blonde hair. Jean brushed it every morning and put it into two long plaits. On her fifteenth birthday Sarah'd gone to get her ears pierced in the salon in the arcade, and, on a whim, let them crop her hair at the same time. When she came home, Jean cried. She'd had it short ever since.

Where she'd been slight as a child, she was sinewy now. She carried herself better, taller. She wore a dark blue Puffa jacket which she'd got in Camden Market, black Levis and an old pair of suede hiking boots. She'd never possessed a pair of proper girl's shoes.

In London, she belonged to a gym. She did kick-boxing and weights. 'It's addictive,' she said, making a concerted effort with Greg, 'you should try it.' All that training had emphasised a line of muscle, thick as cable, from her shoulders to her neck. She said she got withdrawal symptoms when she came home.

Greg knew that Sarah must have known Dave Pilton – everyone did. He was a flash git, right from primary school; he'd got a girl pregnant in year nine. 'Fanny magnet' was what he called himself.

Greg wasn't going to tell her, and yet it was there at the front of his brain like oil on water. Remembering how Claire had persuaded him to go out to Heroes with a gang of the girls from work. She'd promised she wouldn't make him dance: that he could sit and watch them from the bar.

Sitting high up on a black plastic-topped stool, he'd felt precarious. Because of the high rainfall that summer, the basement was full of the stench of the river which ran alongside; the strobe lighting – red, yellow and green – was making his heart race; he'd drunk too much. His limbs juddered when he got to his feet.

Dave was on the dance floor with some of the soldiers from the camp. They were lairy, arms about each other's shoulders. Dave was tall, like a great ape, thrusting his pelvis, arms stretched out, a half-empty glass extended in one hand. And Claire wasn't going anywhere, she was in his orbit, in her white stilettos killing herself laughing, sticking out her tits.

Greg had pushed his way over and tried to scoop her up – a child in a riptide – shouting something into her ear above the throb of the music. But she was shaking her head and pulling away from him: she didn't want to be rescued.

'Suit yourself,' he'd said, enraged suddenly and backing off as all the lights turned red. He made for the exit, walking like you'd walk on a ship that's twisting the line of a wave. Then he groped along the powdery bricks of the wall outside, around the corner, and threw up in a pile of cardboard boxes.

He felt better once he'd been sick; but then he felt worse. He felt like crying. 'Little bitch,' he heard himself saying in a voice that sounded high and unbroken.

'Fancy going out?' Sarah said after a while. Greg looked at her blankly.

'Come on,' she said, getting to her feet decisively. 'We'll go mad if we stay in here.' She arched her back and stretched her arms, as if there was no significance in the fact that this was the first time she'd ever asked him to go anywhere with her.

*   *   *

Though it was never as wild as where they were brought up – which was higher, up on the edge of the moor – it was wild enough. You could hear trees hissing down by the river and the wind whistling up the street like it was blowing across bottle tops. There was a tin can rolling this way and that outside the butcher's. Under each of the street lamps there was a flag of horizontal drizzle.

'Where'd you want to go?' Greg asked.

'Not the Lamb,' Sarah said.

'Let's go up the hill.'

They clenched their arms against their bodies, tucking their hands in under their armpits and burying their chins in the collars of their jackets. At the top, they stamped their feet and pushed through the gold and brown swing door of the Red Lion.

'Freezing down here,' Sarah said, 'bloody freezing,' unwinding her scarf and looking around to see if there was anyone she recognised.

It was always gloomy in the lounge bar. There was the glow from the fire, and spots of fairy lights, enough to see that there were odd groups of people sitting at tables, some of whom swivelled round crossly in the draught from the door.

As soon as his eyes adjusted to the light, Greg recognised Les Bradstock. Les was such a regular he had his own chair by the bar and a polished tankard for his beer. By the shape around the tops of his calves, Greg could tell he was wearing his breeches. His long feet were shod in weird fancy brogues.

'All right?' Les gave Greg a sort of salute with his hand. He was looking Sarah up and down and nodded curtly to acknowledge her. He'd got a prickly blond chin – his moustache was tipped with orange from the tobacco he smoked.

'What're you having?' Greg asked.

'Good of you,' he said, lifting his tankard. 'Cheers.'

'Needed to get out,' Greg said. 'They're driving us mad.'

'Christmas – load of codswallop,' Les snorted.

'Les knew Dad,' Greg said by way of introduction. 'They were at school together.' He tilted his head towards her. 'This is my sister, Sarah.'

'I'm parched,' Sarah said, accepting a glass of cider and lifting it to her lips. 'Cheers.'

Les raised his glass but said nothing, looking askance at her, taking in the jeans, the boots, the hair.

'You can tell you're related,' he said finally, gathering the bubbles from his moustache with the tip of his tongue. Greg was getting hot – sweating from climbing that hill, the heat of the fire.

He wasn't mad about standing talking to Les, not with Sarah there. After Claire had gone, he'd started coming more regularly to the pub. He'd let the barn get squalid – a week's worth of washing-up in the sink, spiders everywhere – and going out was his one way of keeping at bay the inevitable retreat back home. It came soon enough, though: the temptation of being cooked for, his laundry washed and ironed.

The regular crowd in the Lion was at least a generation older than Greg. Trigger, Mac and J.P. would appear together and lap against the bar like a creature with three heads. He'd got into the habit, after a few pints, of letting off about Claire. The impulse even to mention her name was irresistible, like fitting your hand through a hole in a standing stone.

'Carrying on, was she?' Les had asked once. 'Lot of it about.'

Until he voiced it direct like that, Greg had kept the suspicion to himself. But it was there, like a trap in a wood. The way she'd brazen it out, when it was written all over her face. Before, he'd only had to get her in the door of Mick's barn – where they were living together, Greg helping to do it up – and they'd fall on each other, her breath coming in fits and starts like a small wicket gate on its hinge. Now she wouldn't let him near.

It was Dave who eventually came to get her, arriving in his white van. Greg had wanted to hurl a rock through the retreating rear window, crack him on the back of the skull and watch the van career into the ditch and upturn, rolling over, igniting into a ball of fire like you got from an oil well – one that left no trace, no skin, no bone . . .

'The minute you think it, believe me, they're at it,' Les had said, 'sure as eggs. They're all bitches in the end. Stick to the feathered variety, boy – they won't let you down.'

'You left us, then – lure of the city lights?' Les was saying to Sarah.

'I went to college,' Sarah said matter-of-factly.

'Couldn't wait to get away, then?'

'Yep. Soon as I got my chance. That was me: gone.' She shoved her glass along the bar to demonstrate.

'Well done you,' Les said. 'Going to rescue your brother from us?'

'Does he want rescuing?'

'He's had a lucky escape.'

Greg could hear Sarah calling Claire *a man's girl*, like the other girls at school she despised who sat in the common room putting on mascara and lip gloss.

'Saved from a life of slavery,' Les said sardonically.

For a while, it looked as if Sarah and he were getting on like a house on fire. Greg stood as if he were listening, but in fact, as so often happened when he stood in the gloom of the bar with a drink in his hand, he was thinking of Claire.

'Drink?' Les asked him for the second time.

'Sorry. Yes, thanks. Broadside. Ta.' Greg was feeling hot again; he pulled at the zip of his fleece. And if he couldn't quite picture her face, he still kept a photograph of her in his wallet, a passport photo – big panda eyes. When he looked at it he was reminded sometimes of the incongruously harsh things she said: stories she picked up at work, like the time she told him the girls had seen a man jerking off in a window across the road; or how one girl, Sue, was on her second abortion.

When Sarah went to the loo, Les raised his eyebrows and indicated sideways as the door swung shut. 'I'd forgotten you had a sister.'

'Yeah,' Greg said.

'Nice girl.'

'She's all right,' Greg said.

'I never said a word.'

'She lives in London.'

'Enough said.'

Sarah came back into the room. She was smiling at Greg in a way that made her seem for a moment like someone he didn't know. She wiped her hands on the thighs of her jeans and got back up on to the stool, then stood up on the bars across the legs of it as if she were standing forward on a horse, and peered over at the barrels of beer ranged on the floor behind the bar.

'Know your beers, do you?' Les asked.

'I'm not an expert.'

'Did you know there's a beer called Offa's Dyke?'

Sarah kept her position for a minute and then sat back on the stool.

'Strange the names they come up with. In *The Best Beer Guide*, though, this pub,' he said, raising his eyebrows.

'I did grow up here,' she said.

Perhaps it was just the presence of a female among them that made everyone behave a bit differently. Les's skin twitched around his mouth. Greg looked at his sister more objectively, the botched piercing at the top of her right ear, a rim of red that had swollen in the gristly runnel to her lobe like an insect bite.

'What do you do, in London?' Les asked.

'Work for the council. Housing.'

He seemed to consider this, taking a slow slurp of his beer, then he smirked. 'Bet you've got a colourful waiting list.' He snorted. 'Soft touch, this country.'

Greg felt a prickle at his neck and lifted his hand to scratch it quiet. Sarah was staring at the polished chestnut of the bar. She lifted her chin and said levelly, 'Everyone's a right to a roof over their heads.'

'One of the compensations, living down here,' Les went on, 'no coloureds.'

He knew he'd riled her; he had a waiting-game smile on his face.

'Do you want to know why I left this place?' Sarah said, turning on her seat.

'Let's go and get a table,' Greg mumbled, his windpipe tightening. It was him who had to live here. *Give it a rest*, he wanted to say to her.

'Really nice talking to you,' she said, pressing her words down so there'd be no mistaking the irony.

'Up the workers,' Les muttered, lifting his glass to their backs.

'Cunt,' she said under her breath as they reached a table at the far end of the snug. 'Ignorant git.'

Ever since she was a little girl, Sarah had been skinny, Greg had been the plump one. She was skinny and fast. She could run for miles along the sand at Welcombe and he'd never keep up. She was fearless. It was always Greg who kept a weather eye on just how far away they were, making sure he could still see the two dots of their parents' heads against the canvas windbreak. In those days they were both naked on top, wearing matching long safari shorts. When they first arrived, they would skip with their father to the edge of the sea. He wouldn't be hurried, he'd pace it out as if he were conducting a survey. Then he'd stand, knock-kneed, dig his toes into the soggy sand, leaning backwards with his hairy belly as if he were having a wee. Their mother would have taken half an hour to get undressed, directing her husband irritably to shield her from the tug of the wind or from gangs of teenagers pattering and shrieking towards the water. Then she would sit and not move from her spot, leaning out like a rower to sort through the sandwiches and the crisps.

Sarah had found a strip of seaweed and was using it as a whip. She trailed it after her and every now and again, to keep him on his toes, she'd crack a line through the air. Greg was her sea horse. She drove him to the frayed metal edge of the sea. He knew that if she decided to drive him further, he'd have to go. All that would save him were the plans he'd have rehearsed in his head: at the last moment he'd reel away, duck under the waves and tunnel between her legs – even though it meant putting his head under the water – to escape her.

By the end of the day they'd all have changed colour: their father's skin, pallid as greaseproof paper; the bags under their mother's eyes, the tip of her nose, magenta; Greg and Sarah, pink with calamine lotion, like two natives from the same tribe, stinging, smeared in a way that marked them out from every other child on the beach.

Greg was wondering if Les was right about them looking like brother and sister. The school photographs that were kept on the dresser – the peacock blue of their blazers, their stripy ties – where Sarah was forced to put her arms around his waist and said she'd held her head back at that strange angle because she thought he had nits.

'Offa's Dyke,' Sarah tutted indignantly, dipping her fingers into a splash of beer and pushing shapes out of it. 'Did you hear him? So original. So funny.'

'What're you talking about?'

'What do you think I'm talking about?' she said, exasperated.

He saw contained in her face a neater version of their mother: the light green eyes, the weak chin, the nose that had a slight indentation on the end, like a fork mark in dough. These features had been impressed upon him from every angle since he could first recognise a nose, an eye and a mouth, and he had never questioned them. But as he studied her now, like repeating a word over and over, his sense of her suddenly seemed arbitrary, based on nothing but habit.

He was burning: it was something akin to humiliation that she'd caught him out not knowing the meaning of a dirty joke. Or anger, that again, because he was the younger, he was always the last to know. Like when they'd had to move off the farm, or when Gran had had her bowel removed.

He hated her for making him feel stupid. What did he know about girls? He looked at his beer belligerently. Then he said, 'You've been out with boys –'

She groaned. 'Spare me.'

'But you've been out with boys.'

'So you keep saying. It doesn't mean anything. What do you think all the fuss is about?'

'You mean you've told Mum?'

'It's who I am.' She paused and then snapped, 'It makes me sick – you bring home that little slag and it's fine, it's cool. Mum can't get enough of her. Wedding bells. Pattering of tiny feet. And what am I supposed to do? Pretend I'm waiting for Mr Right? For ever? You know,' she continued, 'if you ever had the guts to get out of this dump, you'd look back and think, Christ Almighty, how did I do it? What do you have in common with someone like him?' She made a tiny flip of her eye towards Les. 'Twisted bastard. You'll end up like them. Like Dad.'

'They're not all bad.'

'You've only got to scratch the surface.'

He remembered how she used to tease him, poke his stomach. *Flubber-boy.*

'I'm not like you,' was all he said.

She was on the edge of her seat, hunched over, knitting her fingers together.

'I know that.' But then she said, cajoling him, 'We're not so unalike, you know. Not when it comes down to it. We get hurt. We fall in love.'

Greg flinched. Out loud the word sounded embarrassingly undressed. And yet it sparked in his brain like a wire chewed in an attic.

'If you really want to know,' Sarah said, changing tack impulsively, 'I've met someone.'

It was a while before he registered what she'd said. Her

43

confidences in the past had been rare enough that he could number them: the time she told him that she hated their mother; the pile of rocks she showed him on the moor where she had buried the pink sun hat.

'I'm living with her. She's sharing my room.'

He didn't know what he was supposed to say. Somewhere in the hollow of his head there was an echo sounding, *Claire, Claire.*

'It's the first time – the first time I've been happy in my whole life.' Now she was glaring at him.

He was grief-stricken, panicking. *Claire*: somehow he was holding on to her in the water between him and his sister. One of their endless battles about what was hers and what was his.

'She was an airhead,' Sarah said, picking up her glass and finishing what was left in it, 'forget her.'

He shrugged. Then he said, because it was the easiest and only thing he could think of to say, 'Want another?'

She wrinkled her nose, looking around. 'No. Not here.'

Greg was relieved. She didn't seem to care who could hear her. She got up and pushed her chair in, sauntered over to the bar, standing at the opposite end to Les, who was stroking his tankard, ignoring her. She dug in her back pocket and pulled out some notes to settle up.

'Right?' she said in a new bright voice, turning to Greg.

He fumbled for his jacket. He was looking over at Les, ready to unload an apology. Les didn't flicker.

As they hit the cold air outside Sarah said, 'It's like an experiment: the aliens have been feeding them, drip,

drip, drip, on something that makes them think they're the centre of the universe. They go home, beat up their wives –'

'You can't say that –'

'Whatever the equivalent is.'

The wind had died down, the air so sharp it made their noses run.

'Just look at the sky,' Sarah said. 'You don't get that in London. Wow.'

The moon cast their two bodies behind them, tall as lamp posts, and flooded the sky with a spatter of stars, too many to pick out even rudimentary constellations.

'Spilt milk,' she said. And then she made a sour face, imitating their mother. '*No use crying over spilt milk* – when anything went wrong. *Anything*. She should take a spoon of her own medicine.'

He remembered them sitting in the dark together with the TV on, watching *Star Trek* after school. Their mother would bring them beakers of milk and a plate of marmalade sandwiches.

'That's how I think of it when I come home. Like visiting another planet. I feel sorry for you, Greg. There's more to life.' She ran with a spurt of energy down the hill as if she could barely contain herself, then stopped and turned back to face him as he caught up with her. 'You could come to London. You'd easily find work.'

'Maybe I'm all right as I am.'

'There's plenty more fish in the sea. You're not even bad-looking.'

He was right next to her when she said that, and his stomach contracted.

And then the noise, electronic and insistent, sounded like the *ting-ting* of a bell as if to break them apart. Sarah patted her pocket and pulled out a phone. As she touched it the display lit up her face. There was a message, which she tapped open. She smiled reading it, then slipped the phone back into her jacket.

Greg looked at her.

'Just someone,' she said, tapping her nose with a finger. She skipped ahead of him in her excitement, throwing her head back to address the sky. 'Beam. Me. Up.'

When they got home they could see by the car that their father was back, and it wasn't long before they gathered that Gran had come back with him too.

'One of you is going to have to sleep on the couch.' Their mother fussed in the hallway, taking their coats off them like she did when they came back from school. 'Greg? Mick wasn't there. Do you know what he's up to? Your gran's upset. Not surprisingly.'

Through the door into the lounge, they could see Gran sitting in their father's chair with her coat on and her shiny black handbag poised on her knees.

'I'm too old for this,' she was saying to the room. 'I'm past it. Too old.'

Greg and Sarah followed their mother into the kitchen.

'Talk to your gran,' their mother hissed at Sarah, shooing her back out into the hall. 'Talk to her, make her feel at home.' And then she said to Greg, 'He thought he was having her Boxing Day, that's what he said. Did he say that to you? He knew perfectly well. So why doesn't he ring? You'd think he'd come over and apologise at least. She's his mother!'

'I know nothing,' Greg said and walked back into the lounge.

'Gran? You all right?' Sarah was saying, kneeling down next to her.

'You're a good girl,' Gran said, the skin hanging loosely from her neck. 'I always said you were a good girl. But I'd like to see you in a skirt. On Christmas Day. How about that? Just once. It'd suit you. You've got my legs.'

'That's right, Mum,' their mother said loudly, coming through from the kitchen with a dishcloth in her hands, 'she should show them off more, shouldn't she?'

Their father was shuffling about in his slippers, out of sorts because Gran was sitting in his chair.

'What do you want for your birthday?' he said to Sarah arbitrarily, clearing his throat. 'Two brackets and a plank of wood?'

'Not now, Dad,' their mother said, flashing her eyes at him, watching her grown-up child squatting like she used to on a beach, drawing for herself a giant mermaid. 'You'll only start her off.'

DANCING ON A PIN

They'd worn their band uniforms out of respect, identifiable in their various shapes and sizes by the purple of their jackets, the golden epaulettes. Someone bagged a corner in the dining room and the rest followed as they got their drinks from the bar, bringing over chairs, set to make an evening of it.

'Could have been me – that,' Robert Woodward said, shaking his head. 'Lucky escape.' He said it without embarrassment and he'd looked up to gather approving nods.

There'd been a good turnout for the funeral. The Bradstocks were an old family, going back as far as anyone could remember. The church was full on both sides, and there was a row of extra chairs from the village hall to accommodate the band. Although Dennis had given up playing regularly – too much of a commitment – he'd been happy to be on call if they needed him; a couple of times a year he'd help out in a contest. He was an excellent tenor horn and they'd miss him.

At first nothing was said about Irene, although most of them knew the story. What there was left of her (some had it down to fillings and the studs of her earrings) had been taken off to Exeter awaiting news of relatives.

'Hidden talents, our Dennis. It's always the quiet ones . . .'

The comments came in little forays, nervous about over-stepping the mark.

'Must have been carnage,' one said. 'Bernie told me he'd not seen anything like it – not in his life – wouldn't want to see the like again . . .'

'The only way they knew it were him at the start, that oilskin, melted in the grass like butter – in a pool.'

'Poor bugger.'

It was Robert who brought Irene up. 'She was a big girl,' he said, trying to lighten things, raising his glass as a gesture towards the bar room. 'Lovely smile – nice body.' He nudged Fraser, a young cornet player. 'You know what I'm talking about, don't you?' he said, gesturing with his glass, 'man in his prime like you.'

'Hang on a minute, Bob,' one of the old boys said. 'Life in some of us yet.'

It was hard to imagine that they'd been there on the night, gathered those ten days ago, after playing out in the freezing cold to raise money for the young Watson child, who'd been taken ill over Christmas. Irene had been there behind the bar, ruddy from the fire, her hair pulled back, nothing to betray the fluster as they came in but stray wisps of her fringe sticking to her forehead. That chest of hers, bobbing under, dipping to get the mixers, two lifebuoys, the regulars joked, two plump chickens.

'What're you after?' she'd said, pulling a beer for one customer, addressing Robert.

He got up on to the bar stool, the seat of his trousers pulled down so that you could see the vest coming untucked from his pants, the crack. He shuffled to get his balance, slouched over, looking at her, meeting her eye. His mouth twitched. 'All depends,' he said, 'on what you're off'ring.'

She bent down to check the last drop of bitter into the straight glass in her hand and lifted it to the bar, shaking her head, good-humoured. He was fixing on her, sparkly-eyed, inviting the boys to look and learn.

'Hey,' he said.

'Pint?'

'That'll do for starters.'

She drew the beer from the pump, her bare forearms rippling from the short sleeves of her blouse.

'There you go.'

'Straight up,' he said, bending to meet the glass, licking the overspill from down the side. One of the men spluttered across the surface of his drink, scattering bubbles that caught in his nostrils and eyebrows.

She was used to it. Went with the job. When she was younger she'd have taken it more seriously, she might even have got involved. But now she took it for what it was, let the banter warm her briefly, a game of interest like breath across coals.

It was past midnight when she bolted the door against the last of them and let herself out the back, legs stiff as a table, pulling her coat round. She'd reached the outside edge of town, past the street lights, before he caught up with her.

'Hey,' he called out into the lane. It could have been a tunnel with no end: he couldn't see her, but was aware of movement, six feet or so ahead. She turned and he caught the paleness of her face, a whitewashed wall. She stopped, let him catch her up.

'Hey,' he said softly, more directly. He was swinging a big black case.

She knew it was him, Robert, the butcher from town, the flirty one. She felt awkward with him now, without the bar between them.

'How're you getting home?'

'Walking.'

'In the dark?'

'It's not far.'

Then, chancing his arm, he said, 'Fancy a bit of company?'

She could smell his beery, expectant breath and the way he was already opening up towards her as if he couldn't wait, as if the field would have to do, the other side of a gate, where he'd spread her out on the ground, lumps of wet earth digging into her back. She was lonely and tired, but not too tired to stamp the reflex that urged her, *yes, why not?*

'Not tonight, thanks.'

And anyway, she was thinking, Dennis might come.

(So she hadn't given up hope. There was a trickle of cold water in her head that could shift landslides of shale.)

But Robert was persistent. 'Doesn't it scare you out here – all alone?'

'No.' She was firm as if he'd touched her. 'It doesn't.'

'Coming from a city. Middle of nowhere.'

'No difference to me.' She said it as if she meant it. And it was true, the dark didn't scare her, not half as much as the thought that she'd been wrong about Dennis; that he hadn't really loved her. Stupid, pig-ignorant her for having fallen for the same old story.

She knew she had to keep it together; she'd nearly shaken him off. It was the rich who were really scared – 'shitting themselves' was how her last boyfriend had put it.

'I'm not scared,' she said. 'What have I got to lose?'

Her lack of care was a pinprick.

'Sure you'll be all right?' he said, almost a threat.

'Fine.'

'Another time, maybe.'

Turning slowly, he still imagined she would call him back. 'Wait!' an owl calling. 'Wait, wait –'

He lifted his feet deliberately, tuned only to the silences in between, to the slightest release of hesitation from her. Nothing.

He'd tried. You couldn't blame him for trying. But as he picked up speed, heading for the bright tarmac of the main road, he shook himself. Best thing all round, he thought, raising his face to the spit of rain. He could picture the bottle of Old Grouse waiting for him on the sideboard. Nothing like your own bed.

Drops of rain began to splash heavy, rolling from her cheeks, dangling from the tip of her nose. She could hear him stumbling, unravelling from her. Five days they'd had of it like Noah's flood. She pushed her way forward into the darkness, between the denseness of hedgerows, reaching the point where a sign turned vehicles back, down towards the river, her tights itching with damp, the hem of her skirt dragging. She cursed herself for holding out for Dennis. What was he to her? Something warm to hold on to, that was all.

She blundered across the field to where the river glinted, soaking up wetness from knee-high grass. She was focusing on the scrawny antennae of the aerial Dennis had fixed up, its lines stark against a break in the trees. The caravan loomed in front of her. She fumbled at the door, the close-up judder distracting from the grander sounds of river, the rice-fall of rain. The key was rudimentary. The door only budged when a body's weight pulled on the handle, pressed downwards and then drove in.

Every time she climbed into the caravan, the creak and give of its seams made it seem as if she were stepping on to scales. Already her hand was poised around the matchbox in her pocket. She drew it out and struck a light for the gas ring, not for a kettle, but for the blue and orange colour of it, the need for company.

Earlier she'd bought a big plastic container of oil for the lamp. She reached for it now, but then thought better of it – silly to attempt to pour the oil in the semi-dark; she pushed it away under the sink.

It was impossible to get dry. She rubbed her face and the ends of her hair with a drying-up cloth. Sitting down she turned herself out of her jumper, undid the zipper to her skirt. There was no room! It was exhausting to be so closely contained. Her clothes fell on to the scrap of beige carpet that served as floor. She paused for a minute, took in the familiar smell of damp orange Dralon, and then catalogued for herself, by their various shapes and sizes, the volumes ranged on the shelf above the unit, the sad sum to date of her possessions: a second-hand copy of *Tarka the Otter*, a fat microwave cookbook, a tall Michelin atlas with the spine and the Devon pages missing, three year-old copies of *Hello!* In a week, she'd be thirty-nine. Nearly forty. Where life begins.

It better bloody had: the thought came automatically, a stubborn reflex of optimism. In the same way she let the caravan remind her of the Wendy house her dad had put up in the yard when she and Kate were little – an early Christmas present between them, and they'd fought over the space, just room enough to park two chairs.

Their mother was going to make curtains for them, but it never happened. The yard didn't get the light, and even in summer it was chilly out there. When Kate lost interest and it became indisputably hers, Irene put more effort into making it a home. She filled a biscuit tin with bits of stone and china, the shells she'd picked up on a beach, laying them out in a pattern on the other chair for dinner, for when her husband would come back from his office, kiss the top of her head, for the two little girls they'd have.

Irene shut off the flame and pulled herself up in the dark over the ridge of the back seat, into the nest of rugs that was her bed. Kneeling, she hooked her arm behind, undid her bra, leaving it on under her blouse, and she left her knickers and tights too. They crackled with electricity as she manoeuvred the furry rug over her shins, tucking it down and round with her toes.

Her head was still buzzing from the fug and clatter of the pub, the balloons of faces at the bar. His fleshy lips. At the window the rain sounded like fire, then even heavier, like bullets ricocheting off the tin roof.

There was a physical, bloody loneliness to it that she'd never experienced before. Not the abstract, damp-in-the-wall feeling she was used to, but a peculiar, gaping wound. She put her hand to her stomach, an empty leather bag, all the contents shaken loose. Sometimes she'd imagined a creature inside, curled up, pushing with its knees. Her weight would go up and down. A couple of times in the past she'd been asked by punters whether she was expecting, and had had to laugh it off.

The wind agitated her, brushing branches randomly against the roof and the walls. She could see atoms – red, blue, orange – hanging in the air, thickening around objects, thinning towards the half-curtained window. Perhaps it was that last drink, which she could still taste, that had left her with a sense that she was moving, being pulled along on the open road. Movement infected her dreams. One night she'd woken with a start, sweating, with the caravan poised on the edge of the river to tip her in. Another time she was already there, bobbing along in the thrust of the current, saucepans and plates jangling, beached, miles downstream in the river's mouth, waking to the scream of seagulls.

* * *

Dennis had offered her the caravan in the summer. He'd come back on the coach one time with the band, all the way from a contest in Bugle. They were celebrating, their boxes of instruments cluttering the pub, making it difficult to serve food. Dennis was at the bar, cheerful on his second pint of cider, the novelty of company. When Irene mentioned she was looking for somewhere, he raised his hand. The caravan was standing empty, he said. He and his wife, Alma, had thought they'd do it up, let it out for holidays or fishing, but they'd not got round to it yet. She was welcome, he said. They'd work something out in the way of rent; he'd ask his wife.

She should have moved on ages ago. But it had become a test of her mettle, that she could hack it, and then, when Dennis had started coming round – at first just to sort out the window, put up the aerial – something about the way it contained the two of them, away from prying eyes, made it so easy.

But he hadn't been near for days, and it didn't take long for her to entertain the thought that he might never come back. She scoffed at herself, hugging her knees, for ever imagining that a man could be otherwise.

When it came, she must have been half asleep, because the knock, rapping, urgent, filled her with terror. She said too quickly, 'What! What is it? Who is it?' and she tried to get herself upright, pulling together her blouse, calculating just how quickly she might reach for the saucepan out of the cupboard, how heavy it would be.

The scrabbling at the door was amplified in the drum of

the caravan. Not that man, Robert, come back? When it gave, the door caved in so suddenly that the force of the shoulder behind it drove the man into the room further than he'd intended, dripping in oilskin like a fisherman returned by the sea.

'Dennis?' She dropped back on her heels. 'Dennis,' she said again with relief, everything forgiven. His face glistened in the fragile light of his pocket torch.

'Look how wet you are! Come on then, come in, quickly.'

He lifted the oilskin over his shoulders, shook it, and left it outside by the steps in a heap. Then he climbed up, pulling the door shut behind him, lowering his head sheepishly.

'Worried you'd got drownded, weren't I?' he said.

'Come here!' She had never experienced such gratitude, like an escaped part of herself finding home, clambering down to meet him, her arms outstretched as he shuffled clumsily on his knees, tripping over himself to get to her. The blouse gaped open and the bra, which reminded him of a suspension bridge, fell forward, the indistinct mass of her breasts almost touching her lap.

There were no words. They had rehearsed this, again and again: his life, her life, shed in a clatter of armour; the two of them ready to throw in their lot on a boat they'd rustle up between them; a dovetailing of limbs, assembled almost instantly.

This time, though, she took his head in her arms and brought it to rest across her thighs, pressing him down, stroking firmly the rough hair behind his ears, taking in his smell in small gulps. She held him off, a tiny punishment, holding her breath as she listened to the wind, to the rain, refusing to let go, hovering above him.

She could feel his head pushing up against her hands and eventually she let him free.

'Iren-e,' he whispered, full of apology.

He had no idea how he was going to tell her. Only hours earlier, he'd walked into the kitchen at home and found the table laid: a solitary napkin rolled neatly in his father's horn ring, shepherd's pie, spooned out so that a film had formed over the meat, peas in a clump, ketchup ready, upside down. His mouth had gone dry.

At either side of the knife and fork was an elaborate *placement*: four grainy Polaroids, two each side, a chemical trace like flypaper. Taking them in, top to bottom, left to right, his hand gripped the back of the chair. The images were underexposed but unmistakable: the dirty green of a caravan, the snitch of a window, a crack of curtain, and in the bottom right corner, his oilskin in a heap.

It had Les written all over it. *Jesus Christ.* As if his brother had been born only to torment him. Even after their father died and they'd agreed to split the farm – him, as the elder and married, in the farmhouse, Les down in the bungalow with their mother – it had made no difference. Like certain bullocks, treated just the same as all the rest, but with a mad wall eye, Les would have you soon as look at you.

Dennis throbbed with the injustice of it. Better not to have a wife, he'd want to shout, than a woman who'll not let you near. Lambing time when he'd be half-delirious, three in the morning, still he'd rather be out in the frost with a ewe heaving on her side, the knife-edge of a pelvis bruising his hand, grabbing and pulling, his arm glazed in the warmth of mucus and blood. Sometimes when he went indoors and pulled the blanket over him, it was heavy as the lid of a coffin.

He'd meant to tell Irene straight away, but the words wouldn't come out. When he was young, they'd go to the pantomime. He was scared of the velvet seats, the way they clapped him in their huge, soft jaws. He had butterflies all the way as they drove out of the valley, just like he had now. The hush and glow of the caravan, her cushions, her fluffy rug, her sweet, receptive flesh. Aladdin crouching over his lamp, tipping out gold, everywhere, tipping bright, golden coins from the roots of his being, feast after famine, the huge swill of grain from the silo, the last drop of radiant intoxicating cider, like a raging thirst, and like the opposite of thirst. And he knew then that it would kill him to do without her.

He followed her, scrambling over the seat into the bed, the two of them like mountaineers, falling over themselves to get to the summit.

The way he looked at her, as if she was something special, it undid her. The way he traced with his lips the back of her neck, or chucked her breasts like the chins of orphan lambs. He breeched her so that her whole dispossessed body tautened under his, and the juddering effect she had on him, down to the tips of his feet, pricked the backs of her eyes.

The rain rained on the river, tiny pinpricks of absorption. Dennis buried his head in her, holding on to her as if he would never let go.

When he pulled away and lay on his back, he almost choked on the word.

'Sorry.'

She knew she had to stop him speaking and pulled his head towards her.

'She knows,' he said, muffled. Irene couldn't see his face. 'S'll have to call it a day.'

She breathed heavily, the rain crackling like the end of a record.

Heat radiated through his hair like coils of an electric fire.

'Not your fault,' she said, stroking mechanically, 'knew I was dancing on a pin.'

'Maybe things'll calm down.'

He drew back his head and looked up at her to show that he meant it, and in that small movement she lost her footing, catching hold of him, recklessly.

'Can't you stay?' she said. 'Just a bit? Just this time. It's so dark.'

She was reminded of the times she would lie in bed, far into the morning, floating in and out of sleep. If she could choose, this was how she'd live: before the invention of minutes or hours. Half in a dream, half in the stillness of a room – no need to set foot on the cold lino of the floor. If he would stay, she knew she could fit such a lifetime into his staying.

'I hate the rain,' she said, pulling him to her. 'Don't you hate it?'

Alma had a torch. The night belonged to the torch which traced its way from the farmhouse, lighting the drizzle in snatches of glittery cloth all the way down the track. She was wearing her gardening shoes – boots cut down at the ankles. And although it was impossible to tell, she knew she was following in his footsteps. The red metal can from the shed was three-quarters full and the liquid inside slopped against the funnel of the neck like sea in a cave.

She stumbled as if she were being tugged too eagerly along the path. The track was longer than she remembered, and steeper. When she got to the gate, the ground was waterlogged, churned up from sheep passing through. From over the top she looked across to the river, the straggly, low-lying trees along its bank, and picked out the blunt thumbprint of the caravan. She held the can steady on the top bar and hauled herself up, almost losing the heel from one of her shoes, lowering herself on the other side, her foot pushed home in a squelch of rubber. The cold of the metal bar made her practical. She unscrewed the top from the can and put the lid to rest like a doll's hat on the post; then she found a spot under the hedge for the torch – leaving her a free hand – watching the grass flare in ribbons as she laid it down, tiny ball bearings of light.

She clambered on into the field, clumps of rushes to her knees, the river winking at her through the kaleidoscope of rain on her glasses. The caravan seemed smaller than she remembered, shrunk against a cross-hatching of trees and the pounding of river water, but even in the dark she could detect movement, a gentle rocking, and a dull creaking like canvas sails.

She caught her breath – so close, if it hadn't been for the tin walls, she'd have been in the same room, squashed between them, breathing the same boxed-up air.

'At it,' Les was spitting in her ear, 'hammer and tongs – like rabbits.'

She bit the inside of her mouth to stop the involuntary spooling of home-movie pornography. Then, doggedly, she paced out a semicircle, a mean, bite-sized chunk of land, from the bank of the river around the perimeter of the caravan. She slipped the silky liquid alongside her as she went, sloshing the remains of it underneath, between the wheels, as if she were rinsing the front doorstep.

The sound of the first match striking split the air. It fizzed for a moment against the shelter of her hand, a bright hole in the night, whipped out by a gust of wind. Her hands shook. Les. She could see his teeth, a film of prehistoric mucus glazing every word. She struck again.

This time the flame spurted and furled from her fingers, licking the grass in a bright snake all along by her feet and then streaking in one fell *swhoosh* towards the bank, up and under the caravan. For a minute the night was turned inside out. Darkness scattered to its roots; the river glittered and the air pulsed golden in the mirrors of her cheeks.

She thought she heard a cry and tore herself away, blocking her ears with her hands, hauling herself back across the field as if through high water, intent on the weak projection of the torch. She arrived at the gate in disarray, a crane fly, bashing at the plastic shell of the torch to reactivate its failing light.

It was a furnace in the Red Lion, the yawn of the huge chimney half the length of the room. Ranged around the fire their faces were red and shining, their eyes caught in its bright headlights. One of them was remembering how after Band some nights, Alma used to come looking for Dennis; how you could tell by the way she marched in that she was furious to be caught taking the trouble. She'd keep her scarf on and lift her chin above the sea of heads, the beer mats, her eyes darting towards the place they wrote the menus, over to the games room, twitching her neck like a fishing rod.

'He'll be in for it, tonight,' someone would say, snorting.

It was past midnight when Robert came through, bringing a tray of whiskies which glinted as he set them down.

'Come and see,' they beckoned him. 'See what Les has got.'

Les had been handing pictures round furtively, four or five of them.

'What you got there?' Robert said, climbing heavily over Terry's knees to take his seat.

Les hunched his shoulders, conspiratorial. There was spittle at each corner of his mouth where his breath came shallow like a dog waiting to be fed.

'Little souvenir,' he said.

'Let's see,' said Robert, holding out his hand, expecting something mucky. He felt the sweat break round his ears when he recognised a picture of the caravan, marvelling at how hard-faced Les – Dennis's own brother – could be.

'You taking on the farm?' he asked him, shuffling the pictures absently.

Les shrugged.

'You'd have thought she might move, Alma – something like that happens?'

'I'm fine at Mother's for the time being.'

They would talk of Dennis in the pub a lot longer than they talked of Irene. He was something to them, a piece of the jigsaw of their lives, whose blank edge would give them pause for thought. She was a ship in the night, a summer barmaid, here one season, gone the next. No one even knew if she had family. She was that funny age: you didn't ask questions.

'Look at that,' Robert said, taking a second look, indicating with his thumb the window of the caravan. 'It could have been me, that. In there. Talk of a lucky escape.'

'Poor bugger,' Terry said, shaking his head.

'Never does to mix business with pleasure,' Robert said, raising his eyebrows.

'You'd know about that – eh?' Terry said, chuckling.

'Cautionary tale . . .' Robert said.

'Hope he died happy,' Fraser said, looking around at the others with his tongue in his cheek.

'And the rest,' Les said, putting the photographs back in his breast pocket. 'Dirty dogs.'

LOVE ME TENDER

Les had been out in the woods doing something he shouldn't have, saw the caravan in a blaze and left it a while to call the fire brigade. By the time the men got down there, it was all over. When the sergeant came up to the farmhouse the first time, late next morning, Alma thought they'd come for her. But he was courteous, treading carefully. Sergeant Owens, he'd said, showing her his badge, and a lady in uniform with him, asking when she'd last seen her husband and then – they'd better come in – breaking the news. Did she have family she could call? The sergeant said he could see she was upset and that he'd not trouble her for long: routine: forms that needed filling. He'd make it as easy for her as he could.

The lady handed her a card when they were ready to go; she scrunched her eyes: 'Anything you need, just ask,' she'd said.

The tenor horn had been Dennis's father's before him, kept polished along with the cups he and Les used to win for running. When Dennis had practised – latterly, less and less – he did it up here, balancing music on her dressing table, against the mirror, propping the pages open with her hair-brush.

He'd let her have a go in the months when they first met. They'd laughed about the noise she made. 'Pardon me!' he said like Norman Wisdom every time she pursed her lips and blew, as intimate as they'd got about bodily functions. He played for her then, 'Aura Lee'.

'You'll know this one,' he'd said. She'd shaken her head. 'Wait and see.'

There was a white wooden gauge set in the bank of the river with black marks against it to measure the highs and lows of flood water. Alma woke up numb as wood. Things fluctuated alarmingly. She'd given no thought to being here *after*. The stuff that bubbled up in her mouth: she could have been a child with all the trouble of learning to speak ahead of her, or in her dotage, aware of language like rain in the trees, something she'd lost the knack of.

The second morning, she'd taken the curtains down from the window, to stop him hiding there. It meant that when she woke, she woke abruptly, shoved into daylight blind, as if from a dark hole.

This morning there'd been something else: a disturbed, metallic sound. At first she thought it was a fox or a rat at the dustbins; but when it came again, the sound was so close it seemed to be in the bedroom: a thump at the glass, a hand wrapped in a duster. She patted the bedside table for her glasses and sat propped up, staring hard at the window.

There was a pip-pip-pip outside like a dripping tap. And then again — thud — a clot of red against the pane. She swung her legs over the side of the bed and dangled her feet. *Thud, kafuffle*: there it was, although this time she detected the skittering of clawed feet.

She bent low, peering out towards the window. A thick electric cable ran from the corner of the house diagonally into the trees. And there it was, a bird — a fat bullfinch with a scarlet chest — collecting itself, puffing its feathers and, just as her shadow reached the window, darting off.

It wasn't the first time Dennis had been back. The bedroom door would open of its own accord. She'd hear its hush and creak and wrap her nerves in a whisper.

'Dennis?'

Every time she opened the silence with his name, she made a door for him, a place for him to come through, to return to her, scourged, shriven.

He never spoke. Just the slow brush of breathing in the corridor.

There were other signs. In the front room she'd found three quarters of a slow worm coiled in the hearth, a cobweb caught where its tail had been ruptured. And, fetching milk from the gate, she'd seen a tiny lizard on the path. Something — a beak? — had shot it through the head, its belly either side, panting in and out. Now it was the bird, driving at the window. *Whosoever shall seek to save his life shall lose it; and whosoever shall lose his life shall preserve it.*

She dug her feet into the slippers by her side of the bed and tightened the cord of her dressing gown. There seemed to be nothing she could do to stop the world pressing in.

Downstairs the flagstones were cold even through her slippers. The cat was scrabbling at the window. She drew the top bolt on the kitchen door, lifted the heavy latch to let him in. He yowled at her, arched his back and swept against her legs. She lifted her feet to avoid the contact of fur.

'Wait a minute – just wait,' she said, a catch in her voice, turning towards the sink, reaching for the kettle, filling it with a spurt of water that splashed her front, leaning over from the cat at her feet to park it on the Rayburn.

'Wait.'

She shuffled off to the pantry. The box of dried food rattled emptily.

'You'll get your food.'

The cat was yowling and weaving in and out.

'I said so, didn't I? Leave off.' And then, because he was making her want to scratch her legs, the poison ivy of his fur, she hissed, 'No. Out! Go and feed yourself! Shoo!'

She opened the door and shut it fast after his tail. 'Go away. Leave me alone.'

She'd hardly had a minute to herself when she heard the scrunch of tyres in the yard, saw the polished white and yellow chequers of the police car: Sergeant Owens, back.

'I'm not dressed,' she said at the door.

'Don't you worry, Mrs Bradstock, we've seen it all before.'

He liked the sound of his own voice. People didn't have

the sense they used to, he was saying. Old-fashioned combustibles, they don't realise what they're handling.

'It seems, Mrs Bradstock, from our information, there were two of them, in the caravan. Does the name Irene Swinton mean anything?'

They'd been through this before, she was sure.

'Irene, yes – I didn't know her second name – the girl from the pub. I didn't know her really. But she was – staying there.'

And did she – Mrs Bradstock – know anything about a red container – metal – for liquid? For paraffin perhaps? It was important. The best lead they had at the moment.

No idea, Alma said.

Did she mind if they took a little look around the outbuildings? Anything missing?

Dennis and Les, they used the sheds, no one else.

Could anyone else have had access to them?

Not as far as she knew. The dog was kept locked up at night, but he'd have barked. No. Nothing. No one.

Would she mind dropping in at the station? Signing a statement?

She would get dressed. She was going into town anyway, later, to do some shopping. Would it be all right if she came then, less fuss?

Absolutely, Mrs Bradstock. Quite all right.

Dennis had stood before her and the notes began to arrive, whole and perfectly placed, great blossoms, in the air. And he was right, she found herself humming, matching words to the tune: 'Love Me Tender'. Of course she recognised it, and, despite herself, she appeared to know all the words. Though she'd have never admitted it, even she had been stirred by Elvis, the squeeze of his legs, the way he sang to a girl on a swing. Somehow though, without words, with no face, no body, no Elvis, the notes sank deeper, more beseeching, so that, as she listened to Dennis, right through to the end, she was thinking, she could spend her life with a man who played like that.

She pulled the horn out of its case and held it on her knee. How cold it was and awkward. She remembered some nights, his body next to hers, the iciness of her sweats, the way he seemed to recoil from her.

His first kiss – her first kiss ever – a hopeless invasion of teeth: the taste of metal in her mouth that lingered halfway down her chin where he had slipped, a raw red rash around her lips, which she couldn't disguise from her mother. His eyes had been closed, hers wide open, unfocused, her glasses knocked upwards, off kilter.

It was the aftershave in that kiss, the same aftershave that gave him away. After twenty years in the bathroom cupboard, the reek of Old Spice had crept back into their lives, slapped into his cheeks these last few months before he went out in the evenings.

She hadn't banked on the way the world would come knocking for her. After the police, it was the vicar, Mr Grayson. Alma was on the flower rota, she'd hardly missed a Sunday in her life.

She'd given him a glass of elderflower wine, two years old. It tasted of cat, she knew. But he drank it and complimented her. He was getting fat, he hardly fitted the kitchen chair. He said he was sorry he hadn't come straight away. Would she like him to say a prayer?

He'd taken her hands and turned them to stone.

Dear Lord, look down on Thy servants we beseech you, and protect those – our dear late friend and husband as was, Dennis Bradstock – who enter Thy Kingdom, where we shall meet again and have eternal life . . . Amen. He'd hung his head.

If she had grasped one thing, it was that she was in the *after*, the ever *after* where there'd be no rota, no Sunday mornings.

'It's in Luke,' she said, looking at the ceiling. 'The two men in the bed: *The one shall be taken, and the other shall be left.* What does it mean? To say the one shall be left?'

Mr Grayson could see she was disturbed. She was in a rather grubby dressing gown, her hair hardly combed. He adopted his thoughtful, charitable face.

'I shall have to look that up. Luke, you say. Thank you. I'll make a note.' He set down the little pink glass and sucked his lips.

'Lovely, that. Just what the doctor ordered,' he smiled, 'though don't tell anyone I said that, will you? Now,' he said, rubbing his knees to get himself up off the chair. 'Old bones,' he said, and then, as if getting down to business, 'Will you join us on Sunday? It might cheer you up – you're always welcome, you know that. In God's House.'

*   *   *

The case was kept under the bed, and these past few afternoons Alma had made something of a habit of going up to the bedroom and pulling it out. She'd lift the lid and stare straight down into the throat of the silver funnel.

When she pursed her lips she tasted petrol. She sat up and drew a deep breath into her stomach like he'd told her, pushed it out through clenched lips: a doleful foghorn. Again, from the depths of her, the quaver of a voice: *bah, bah, bah*. She stopped for a moment, her head swimming, and then took another deep breath, pushed: three wobbly notes ascending.

If she could only teach herself, then he'd come back. If she could just get through that song, 'Love Me Tender', like a quiet spell, he'd be there, she could feel him already, the soul of him warming the metal.

When she'd had enough, she'd take the instrument and lay it beside her carefully on his side of the bed. Then she'd lie with her nostrils to the rancid breath of the mouthpiece, one hand to keep it there like an iron lung.

After the police had been, her heart had fluttered to the surface. Although it never got warm in the kitchen, even with the Rayburn, she was sweating. She lifted the edge of the net curtain. Les had been skulking around as he did most days, working outside. What did she know about livestock? She knew that he was only biding his time. Rex, who'd looked at her accusingly with his tail tipped to the ground, had taken himself off, probably back at the bungalow with the other dogs where he'd be fed.

Alma sat down. The table was cluttered with papers,

veterinary reminders, forms to be filled, phone bill, electric. She pushed the muddle back with the side of her arm. Where she'd left the lid off the dish, the butter had been scored by the cat's tongue. There was a pile of dirty cups and saucers, one supporting a lichen-coloured mould, another with a fly bobbing like a knot of sodden wool.

She hadn't heard the car arriving, and before she had a chance to think a door slammed conclusively in the yard, and footsteps came tapping, little ones, tot-tot-tot, tot-tot-tot. Alma panicked, got herself on to the floor, down under the table, pulling in her head, drawing the dressing gown close around her. Tot-tot-tot, the footsteps stopped. There was someone at the window, sponging a circle for a mouth.

'Alma. Alma, dear. Can you hear me?'

It was Iris, her voice like a drill. The third time she'd been round in as many days.

'Alma – just popped over to see how you are? I've something to leave you. Cats'll have it else. Can I bring it inside?'

It was an old trick: a present for a child. This time, Iris sounded as if she wouldn't be leaving; she was on tiptoe, stretched up. She couldn't have seen right into the kitchen, not possibly, and yet her words found Alma out, touching her like the backs of spoons on her skin.

'Alma. Alma, dear. We're worried about you.'

Her breath was misting the window as fast as she could clear it. Then she seemed to drop down, collect herself. On the embossed lino, Alma breathed through her gills, in, out. But a moment later she heard fumbling at the back and with a jolt, realising that she'd left the door unbolted, shot up, banged her head on the ceiling of the table.

'Alma?' Iris was peering around the kitchen door. 'There you are!'

Iris bustled towards her as if her presence under the table was of no consequence.

'I've got something,' she began again, still not able to see her properly, holding out a light blue Tupperware box.

'I made a big batch, thinking of you – cheesy ones – hope they'll be nice.'

Alma's face boiled. She pulled herself up by the chair, pushing wads of hair behind her ears, snatching the front of her dressing gown.

'Alma, dear, you don't look well. Shall I put the kettle on?' Iris said. 'Can I make you a cup of something?'

'I'm all right –' Alma said, mumbling. 'If you don't mind, I'll just go up, get myself dressed.'

'There's no need on my account. Not for me. Not if you're poorly.'

'I must get up. Got to go out – in a minute.'

'Get yourself shipshape, then. I'll make us some tea.'

Alma caught the smell of herself leaving the room, smeary and sharp. When she got to the landing, she shot into the bathroom and turned the key. She let out a puff of air, holding fast to the doorknob, then shook off the dressing gown. Her thin nightie was wet and cold where it touched her sides. She caught sight of herself in the cabinet mirror: the coat hanger of her neck and shoulders, the smudged rings around her eyes, the yellowish drop of her jaw. And her hair, a fright, dust-coloured and so dense that when she pressed it down it sprang back, out of control like the grass around the house, everything growing with abandon since he'd gone, right down to the claws of her toenails, which even at the best of times she neglected. (She remembered how she'd caught him once in bed, scratching a line sharp as a bramble down his shin that had made him cry out in the night.)

When she got downstairs, Iris was clearing up.

'Well,' Iris said, twisting round from the sink, 'that's better.'

'Iris, don't bother, please. I'll do that. I'll do it later.'

'It's no trouble. You need a bit of looking after, I can see that. Shock you've had.'

'There's no hot water. Immersion's gone.'

Iris took no notice, holding a pile of saucers between her hands.

'You've got to let us help. We want to help, dear. That's what we're here for.'

Alma was wrung out. Iris was squat, wide as a barn. Her cardigan was pinned with a brooch of marcasite flowers, her skirt a trunk of beige.

'Have you been eating properly? You must eat?'

'I'm going into town today.'

'I can always get you bits? You've only to say. No trouble for me to add to my list.'

'Good for me to get out.'

Iris brightened. 'That's right. Lovely spring day. Now. Have one of these.'

She peeled off the lid and held out the box of scones, giving it an encouraging jiggle.

'They've turned out fine, haven't they? Try one.'

Alma reached politely.

'Have another?' Iris said immediately, shuffling them again. 'Go on, there's plenty.' Then she set the box on the table. 'Look, I'll put them down here and you must help yourself.'

The way the light didn't come straight into the kitchen but filtered in green, brown, river colours. The way she imagined a grandmother would be, the grandmother of fairy tales. Warming the pot. And her, sitting on a high stool, swinging her legs, having a biscuit from the jar, ankle socks all washed and ironed, so clean they'd never get dirty again. Granny, cooking by magic, over and over, and *come and sit on my lap, my pet*, her soft warm bosom, the cotton flowers of her dress, her permanent cardigan, the click of things being made.

Iris was sitting chewing on her back teeth, looking from under her spectacles at a beetle-sized hole in the lino on the floor. The crumbs in Alma's mouth were big as stones. Iris raised her head.

'Been a terrible shock to you – for everyone. I don't suppose you've been sleeping? Go to the doctor,' she urged. 'That's what he's there for.'

She licked a crumb from the corner of her lips and squashed it against the roof of her mouth, swallowed.

'He'll give you something. Something to take the edge off. Help you sleep. You'll feel a lot better.'

The hubbub of the kettle, which Iris had filled again for washing up, was dwindling to a hiss. Apart from the clack of Iris's chewing, they sat in silence. For a moment, Alma entertained a vision of herself disguised in scalding water, her skin blistered to brocade. When she poured the kettle into the sink, steam brushed her face like a cobweb.

'Did I ever tell you,' Iris said suddenly, 'about the convict?'

Alma was holding tea cups, dipping them into the boiling water by their handles. She shook them and brought them over. Iris lifted the pot and poured the tea.

'Not the whole story,' she said, 'I've never told anyone that.'

'There's no milk,' Alma said.

'Never mind.' Iris was undaunted. She settled herself, making a fuss of her teacup, placing it, precisely, in front of her.

'He was off Dartmoor. They had helicopters out.'

She took the cup and raised it to her nose, but felt the fire from it, and put it back on the table. 'It gave me a terrible turn. Worse, you know, than I ever let on.'

Alma had no space for stories but she sat and let the words fall about her like chaff.

'Everyone was out. Bank holiday – a day of it. Everyone but Father – who was working – Mother, brothers, sister. Just me at home. I had troubles down there – terrible, for years – I wasn't myself. Not up to a long walk. Mother said, "Sure you'll be all right?" "Yes," I said, "right as rain." It always took me bad, the first day or two.

'I was up in my room. With a bit of embroidery – I never

finished it – I ached and ached and my mind wasn't on it, not at all. Then I heard the door. I thought, that'll be Alan back. No stamina – he was only nine or ten at the time – the baby. I think I even called out, "Alan? Up here!"

'He came. I heard every creak on the stair. But when the door opened, what a shock. It was a man, high as a wall. Unshaven, dark hair. And his clothes were muddy, a dirty ring right through his ear; his fingers caked and black like he'd been hit with a hammer. I couldn't speak. Not a word.'

Iris sat with the flowery cup held stiffly in front of her.

'He stood right there. And I remember I couldn't shut my mouth. He started laughing. Very quiet, but laughing. "Something to show you," he said.'

Alma was listening now, her mouth slightly ajar, her tongue floating.

'I thought he'd come to kill me,' Iris said, 'the way his hand dug around in his pocket.' She took a sip of tea that made her wince, and then, looking straight into the middle of the room, she hurried on in a little racing voice.

'He did pull something out.'

Alma gritted her teeth. Iris was too far gone in the story to stop.

'I was all crooked up, leaning away, but he was right there. Maybe my eyes were closed, but I could tell he was right in front of me. When I felt him bend down – his breath – he took my hand.

'He made me touch. He held my hand with his and he held so tight it burned. He was saying, "Do you like that? Do you like to touch that?"'

84

'We heard the dog then. My little dog. I don't know where he'd been, but he came in through the garden. He must have heard something. He came making such a racket on the stairs, the man took off, cursing, tripping. There was such a stench, worse than anything I've ever known.' Iris's face crumpled like a child's.

Alma said nothing. She looked over to where Iris was sitting, the spill of noise stopped, sagging in the chair like a vacuum cleaner turned off.

Iris took another gulp of her tea, which seemed to revive her.

'You think no one knows – or no one cares. Men, you see. I know that he was a bad man, but – but sometimes I think they can't help themselves. It's how they're born.'

Alma didn't have to be told how disgusting men could be.

'I don't mean Dennis. I've known Dennis since he was at school. He was a good boy. It's just, sometimes, even the good ones – they can't help themselves.'

So clearly *two men*, Alma was thinking. How strange it was in repose, curled up between the drawstrings of his pyjamas: bald, lazy-eyed, Dennis and his little man. As if she didn't know quite well what that story had meant, the fire and brimstone. *Two men*: one, the man she'd married, undefiled, *Love Me Tender*; the other, like the Book warned, *a gift of incontinency*.

'I know he wasn't like that,' Alma said.

'That's right, dear. He wasn't, not really.' She was stuffing the rest of a scone mournfully into her mouth, nudging stray crumbs with her knuckle. She sniffed and coughed. 'Pardon me,' she said.

When Iris got to her feet, her left hip was aching. She left Alma at the kitchen door, walking unevenly to where her white Mini was parked in the yard. It was awkward dropping herself down to get into the seat. She pulled the door shut on herself and with a sigh took in the reassurance of the dashboard, the silver circle of the speedometer, the engine when it spurted into life, the fuel gauge, hovering as it always did on empty.

For a while, Alma stood as the wash of Iris's leaving subsided all the way along the track. But as she turned to go in, her eye was caught by something on the ground, a glimpse of red like a strawberry under a leaf. She looked up to the dark slate ledge of the window at the side of the house – her bedroom window – and down to where the body lay, turned stiffly towards her, two stark claws thin as bootlaces, the neat stitches of its eyes. *Dennis*.

Something leaked from between her legs, not bathwater, not blood. She turned to go in, shut the door, shot the bolt. Time had slunk back in, the bright red egg timer, the hourglass of sand. She sat on the stairs holding on to the solidity of the banister. She wanted to defecate, to vomit, she wasn't sure which. She climbed up the maroon and yellow of the stair carpet, sickly sweet and soft with filth, followed it, crawling along the landing. She was still crouched when she entered the bedroom, level with the underneath of the bed. There was no room for her to crawl in completely. She began to pull: the black case for the horn, a blue suitcase on wheels, one of Dennis's good shoes, silver in the creases across the toes. And then, as far as she could reach, she extended her fingers for the cool metal of the petrol can she knew was there. It crinkled as she took hold of it, the red of its chest stamped *Marshall & Co.*, deep planetary rings around its neck where a lid, a little red cap, could be screwed in place.

The walls of the can were thin and clanked. Alma hugged it to her, got up off the floor and headed for the window. The frame was stiff with old paint, a deposit of flies on their backs. She thrust at the casement with the long metal catch at right angles like a poker. When it gave, she lifted the can and hurled it as far as she could, a spin that took it around the corner of the house, out into the middle of the yard. It skipped and clattered across the cobbles, driving an upshot of pigeons and crows from the trees, in a din that told the whole story and made sure that it was spread around for miles.

TESTING

Wendy was on her bed, slumped and looking blankly at the dress that hung from a hook on the back of her bedroom door. The carnival was six months ago, when happiness had been the elation of being elected Queen, the ritual of being fitted out, standing on a chair like a bride so that the hem could be pinned and ironed into place. The mauves of the dress still shone, darkening in the creases and folds as if the material were liquid.

It was after Carnival that Wendy started to do Saturday nights waiting tables in the Red Lion, and then extra sessions over Christmas when it got busy; and it had been Nigel who'd shown her the ropes: how to work the till, how to bottle up mixers. He was twenty-three and lived with his mother at the top of the village. Wendy had been aware of who he was, growing up, but to her he'd always looked the same, as if he'd been born with that receding hairline, arms thin as rope, skin pale as the mushrooms Phil, her stepdad, once tried to grow under the stairs.

'Well done, maid,' Nigel had said to her one Saturday, when the pub was heaving – a darts dinner, a stag night – and she'd been drafted in to work with him behind the bar, dealing with orders thick and fast, shuffling around in the narrow space so that now and then inevitably they were pressing up against one another. It had happened inch by inch, that familiarity, and then something had switched in her head, something that made her life before seem empty.

'Lack of concentration,' Miss Shepherd had told her mother, Linda, at the parents' evening after mocks. 'It's a shame. She could do well if she tried.'

School seemed like Toytown to Wendy now.

'You used to like English? Reading. What's gone wrong?' Linda was tapping a fingernail on the table top.

'Boys.' She glared at Wendy who was splayed in the plastic chair, turning away from her, staring at the floor.

'I've told her, if it interferes with school, it's gonna stop. You need your qualifications.' And then, appealing to Miss Shepherd, 'Doesn't she? Things is different now.'

'Wendy could do very well if she applied herself.'

At first Wendy had delighted in clearing a space on the shelf above her bed for her set texts: *Far from the Madding Crowd*, *The Crucible*, *Much Ado about Nothing*. They were proper books with proper names, books that made her mother think she was cleverer than she had been. But the glow had worn off. Now all she saw when she opened them up were the scrawls of other people's notes. Someone had written in biro, *irony?*; another: *boredom* and *crap*. There was nothing new to find out. Words were dry as dust compared to life.

Wendy wore the blue fleece he'd left behind one time, relishing the way the long arms contained hers right to the ends of her fingertips, playing with the zip, pressing her nose against the shoulder, sucking the smell of him into her breathing. When he wasn't with her, the world stopped. And the more she yearned for him, the more she hated her mother; the more she hated her mother, the more she yearned for him. She'd shut herself in her bedroom. Her tongue was thick and swollen with crying.

'He didn't touch me,' she'd yelled from the landing, 'he didn't lay a finger on me.'

Linda was flying down the stairs. 'I'm ringing the pub. We'll get to the bottom of this, believe me.'

'I'm sixteen.'

'Not under my roof.'

'You can't stop me.'

'I'd never have known, would I? Sarah's mum had no idea what I was talking about. Camping! And yes, I can, long as you're under my roof I can.'

'He won't be there –' Wendy said, hopelessly.

Linda had no intention of using the phone. But it was a useful trick. *I'll ring your dad*, she used to say. *You can go and live with him.*

'And if you were going to start mucking about, why didn't you take precautions? Don't they teach you nothing at that bloody school?'

'He didn't touch me.'

'So what's this, then? You been testing the cat? We got kittens, have we?' Linda was brandishing the paper bag she'd found in Wendy's bedroom.

'None of your business.'

'Yes it is, I think you'll find – long as you're here, under my roof.'

'I'll go then. I'll leave. I can't stand it here.' Wendy's voice became a sob of rage that rose in the air like a machine taking off.

'Where you gonna go? Come down here!' Linda pushed herself out from the banisters, extending her arms to bring her head into the void of the stairwell. 'And don't screech like that.'

'Fuck off and die.' Wendy turned on her heel and ran into her bedroom, slamming the door behind her.

Linda pounced up the stairs two at a time and began to beat against the door with her fist. 'You little bitch. Don't you dare speak to me like that. Wait till Phil gets back. Open the door, this minute.'

Wendy wedged her foot against the jamb. She clenched the handle, feeling it move minutely under the pressure of her mother's hand.

There was a pile of CDs on her bedside table, and the portable player she'd had since she was thirteen. James Blunt, Coldplay, Lily Allen, Justin Timberlake. She pressed play. *Marching On*: Nigel had given it her, Buckleigh Silver Band: One Hundred Years. Nigel was only seventeen when it was recorded, his face on the cover the size of a pea in the back row. Her mother hated it, called it a racket. Wendy turned the volume up.

School had finished weeks ago, and since Nigel, Wendy had stopped seeing most of her friends. None of that gang would have been seen dead hanging round the band; the boys who played at school were creeps and retards: those sad uniforms, the way they had to march up and down like Dad's Army.

But any trace of derision Wendy might have felt had long evaporated. 'Feelings'. Dennis Bradstock was playing the solo. It was Dennis that got burned to death with the woman who used to work in the bar, Irene. Nigel said that he was the best tenor horn they'd had, a natural – and that particular song had won him best player one year down in Cornwall. The song brought tears to her eyes. Feelings. She turned the volume up again. *Listen and learn*, she thought bitterly, imagining downstairs her impervious bitch of a mother.

Nigel had asked her to Bugle with them for the contest – there was space on the bus. They sat together near the back. Apart from Wendy and a couple of the wives and kids, everyone was kitted out in jackets exactly the colour of the foxgloves which tottered high from the hedgerows all along the route out of town, waving them off with their little purple flags. Julie Westaway and Tracey Fairchild were in the seat behind. They'd been a few years ahead of her at school. Tracey had brought a bottle of cider, which she was offering round. 'Oil the pipes,' she was saying, and then, to Wendy, 'No need for you to hold back.'

Wendy had got up on her knees to talk to them. They were wearing black bow ties like the men. But they had proper handbags and nice hair, and they were friendly – not like at school – urging her to take up an instrument.

'Robert'll teach you. It's free. Go on. It's a laugh. Could do with a few more girls.'

It was a whole new crowd and the novelty made her forget the distance she'd put between herself and the set she'd grown up with – through primary, through secondary – whom she'd erased quietly like footprints in grass.

That day, when Buckleigh took their turn under the blue and white marquee, she'd sat in the audience among members of the other bands and their fans. Nigel had his back to her, in one of those folding chairs, hair tufted from the bus seat, close-cropped at the neck. Wendy was able to pick out Tracey and Julie, Stan from the garage – 'lollipop man' when she was small – Robert Woodward, Bill, blowing into his euphonium to warm it up, adjusting the instrument like a grandchild on his knees. Some she didn't recognise, drawn in from outside Buckleigh, but most of the young lads she knew by sight, most of the older men.

She was nervous for them. Like an exam, the terrible anticipation as the second hand climbs the gym clock. Lips licked, dried with a cuff, and re-licked. Then the baton was raised, pricking a precise spot in the air which a second or two later elicited a swell of sound, rising above the crowd and hovering like a great air balloon. It was impossible not to be caught up: the percussion driving the engine, tickety-tack, tickety-tack, and the chairs and the music stands, bits and pieces of the paraphernalia that would eventually carry them all off, as if they were sailing to a new country, full of hopefulness and common purpose. In the sun, the instruments glinted discs of silver, attached to their players at the lips, a set of antiquated pieces of breathing apparatus, whose efforts, like the tribal songs of colossal mammals, kept the world afloat.

Wendy had been itching to tell him, but made herself wait, to be sure. She'd taken the bus to Exeter the day before, gone to the big Boots, where no one knew her. She did the test in the loos behind the bus station. Almost instantly the line showed blue as she knew it would. She'd hand it to him like a magic wand. Watch his face.

Nigel used to come round and see her on Mondays, his only night off. She would text him when the coast was clear. Linda went to aerobics at seven and Phil, less fussy about who she took upstairs, would be sitting with the papers, telly on, deaf to the world.

Up in her room, they'd be side by side against the wall on her bed. Nigel would spread his warm hand on her thigh and they'd sit like that for what seemed hours, listening to her CDs, before he'd find the courage to stroke her and then to reach behind her ears and kiss.

'Not here,' she'd said, when, after a couple of weeks, he'd begun to position his leg over hers, 'not with him downstairs.'

She wanted Nigel to take her home, to meet his mother – mostly because he seemed reluctant to. His mother wasn't well, he said. She didn't like meeting new people.

'But,' Wendy said, 'I'm your girlfriend now, aren't I? And anyway, I'm not "new".'

'I know,' he said. 'You'll meet her properly, but not this minute. Later.'

'Can we go somewhere, then, just us, where we can be together?'

It was Nigel's idea. He had a tent from when he did the Ten Tors, and there was a farm he knew on the other side of the moor. Wendy could tell her mother she was staying over at a friend's.

Late afternoon on a Saturday in June, they were driving in circles, somewhere near Widdecombe, and Wendy was jumping up and down on the seat cross-legged, saying she wished they could be lost for ever. It was raining; it seemed to have rained all year. The farmer's wife, when they arrived, seemed bad-tempered. She pointed out the pitch by the river from the kitchen window, looking them up and down.

'No rubbish, mind. No loud music.'

Nigel bought eggs to placate her. He called her Mrs Hencott and bowed and scraped like he did to customers in the pub.

They sat in the car until the rain eased off and then made a dash to put up the tent, crawling inside when it was done, not sure what to do next.

'This is home,' Wendy said, the light coming through the yellow walls as if they were living inside a lantern. The pattering on the nylon was like tiny footsteps. She unrolled and spread out the sleeping bags. Nigel reached for the four-pack of lager and cracked one open for her, one for himself.

'Cheers, maid.'

They both took a swig, Wendy tipping it so that the bubbles backed up into her nose.

'Easy,' he said, rolling back on his haunches and watching as she made a show of pouring the last of it down her neck, a party trick – swallowing without even tasting. She brought the empty can down on the groundsheet and it toppled over. She shook her head and blinked. Slowly, shyly he began to strip the top layer of his clothes, and she took his lead, keeping pace. They could hardly move without bumping into each other, wriggling on their backs to get out of their wet jeans.

'Rain's gone right through,' Wendy said, sitting up to lift her darkened T-shirt, her arms in a figure of eight over her shoulders.

When she was down to her bra and knickers she sat back on her shins, her hands clasping opposite shoulders, shivering.

'You're very pretty,' he said, and he reached out to touch a stray line of wet hair. His waxy chest was fluttering, the two pinks of his nipples like embroidery knots. He put the palm of his hand to her arm so that she rocked.

'We don't have to,' he said. 'Only if you want.' Everything he said was in a Devon accent like an old man. 'We don't have to do anything.'

She said nothing but smiled, biting the skin of her bottom lip.

He had brought out a small foil square from his pocket and held it between his hands.

'Where'd you get that?' she asked, as if maybe he was more used to this than he'd let on.

'Somerfield,' he said. 'Died when I got to the checkout

– thought I knew the lady. Bought some milk and an orange to cover it up.'

'Did you – know her?'

'No. False alarm.'

He was kneeling beside her. She watched him bring out the flat, thin circle of rubber she'd seen in a Health Education lesson where Miss Butcher had pulled it about, stretched it defiantly like a children's entertainer. Wendy lowered herself, pressing into the foam mattress, feeling the keel of her back against the ground. Nigel turned away, busy, pulling down his pants so that they circled his thighs. When he swivelled round to face her again she had to look.

'He's in his raincoat,' he said uneasily, watching her expression.

'His mackintosh,' she said, though she was beginning to think then that maybe something wasn't right. She looked steadfastly at the sagging apex of the roof where two or three midges were circling each other.

Nigel manoeuvred to lie alongside. His eyes were set in concentration. He kissed the tip of her nose forcefully and lay woodenly against her.

'Are you all right?' she asked.

Nigel said nothing.

'It doesn't matter,' she said, not knowing what she meant by it. But she put her arm out. 'Come here,' she said. 'It's all right.'

She remembered thinking then that it was almost better if there was something wrong with him, because then he'd be so grateful to her, he'd stick with her. She lay holding his fingers all night, waking every half-hour or so, listening to the outside breathing, the constant chug-chug of the river.

At five in the morning the crows were cawing full blast and the walls of the tent were golden. They got up, bleary-eyed, and peered out of the flap. The world was wide awake – the sky scrubbed to the sheerest blue. She hunched beside him, wearing his socks, his T-shirt and his fleece, as he tried to light a fire.

She hadn't wanted to go back. She was crying next to him in the car, silent ribbons down her cheeks like slug trails. He needed to get home to his mother, he said, check she'd had her medication.

'Why can't I meet her?' Wendy asked reproachfully.

'Don't spoil it,' he said.

'I'm not. I'm just asking. Why not?'

'She's ill, I've told you. It gets worse and then it gets better. Let's just wait until she's up to it.'

'Do you think she'll like me?'

'Course she will.'

'Have you taken other girls to meet her?'

'No, I haven't.' The words were deliberate. He was beet-root and his voice tight when he went on, 'The girl I take to meet my mother – well,' he said, 'that's the girl I'll marry.'

It was way beyond her expectation; her blood turned to warm milk.

'Ten minutes,' Nigel said. He'd turned off the main road

at Okehampton. She didn't ask. The trees made a tunnel on either side and at the end he turned off again, up the army track, drew into an empty car park, next to an old shooting hut. He made no move to get out. From where they were sitting they could see the brim of the reservoir which was suspended high above them, water sheering down a thirty-foot drop like icing on a cake. Without turning to him, she took his hand.

'Look at that,' he said. 'We'll climb up there one day, if you like.'

'Do people jump?' she asked. 'It looks so inviting somehow.'

'I knew a woman did. Someone's mother. She was in pieces at the bottom, broken bones – but they found her before it was too late. It was the last thing she wanted. She's still alive, in a wheelchair.'

'I'd jump,' she said, 'if anyone ever tried to stop us –'

'No need for that,' he said squeezing her hand, 'we'll be all right.'

'Do you really think that?'

'Course I do. You and me.'

She was listening to 'Crazy Little Thing Called Love', an arrangement that required the entire band at one point to down their instruments and click their fingers. She turned the music down for a minute. Radio Devon gabbled from the kitchen and then she heard the clatter of cutlery, the dishwasher unloading. She crept out to the bathroom and locked the door gently. She was having to go to the loo way more than usual. When she got up to inspect the bowl, there was that same sour, tart smell to her pee like beer slops.

It had been nearly seven weeks since her last period. In the bedroom mirror she sat and weighed her burgeoning breasts in her hands, watched her eyes blink back at her, dark with information.

She texted him: *I luv u*, and inserted a smiley face.

It was nothing to do with the camping, she wanted to yell down the stairs. Get your facts right. But ever since then, when she and Nigel met in her house, and rehearsed again, getting a little further each time, they'd become more expert. She saw what she'd always imagined she'd see: what girls had joked about in the changing rooms – cacti, sea cucumbers. In July, in the daytime, often there'd be no one else in the house when he dropped by. His pale green eyes, she could read them like Morse code.

And now, anywhere she went, shops, breakfast, bath, in front of the telly, in the car, wherever, it was all she could think about: the next time. When he wasn't there, she'd reassemble him like a jigsaw: his salty ears, the chocolate button of a mole inside his elbow, the moonlike skin of his thigh. Sometimes, after Band, he'd call in to say goodnight on his way home, the purple imprint of the trombone still in place around his lips like blackcurrant juice, and on the doorstep he'd silently fit his mouth over hers, delve between her teeth so she could taste metal.

She had to tell him now before her mother did. There'd been no response to her message. She picked up the phone and began to fiddle with the settings, his face peering from where she'd set it as her screensaver.

She used her thumb: *Well?* she texted impatiently. Then she laid the phone down on the bedside table and watched it. She was a cat with a mouse. *Where are you?* It was nearly four.

And then – she couldn't help herself – she snatched it up and rang him.

It's me. I need to talk to you.

Before he had a chance to say goodbye she'd cut him off. He'd been cold, formal. She threw the phone on to the bed.

Can I ring you back? he'd said. *Is it urgent?*

It would be different when he knew. They'd be in the hospital, her flat out in a white gown, peering over the range of her belly, him at her side clutching her hand. Their heads would be fixed on the black and white screen, bubbling with expectant smiles, waiting for the nurse and her gliding arm to draw the picture for them.

It was the first step, throwing out a line that he would take and haul her in by: a pink umbilical cord strong as steel, a pram in the hall, a place where she would be the mother – and so unlike her own, it wouldn't be true.

I WISH MY WIFE WAS THIS DIRTY

Phil took the packet of sandwiches he'd made the night before, shut the fridge and went to fill the Thermos.

'Maybe you should try talking to her,' he said, attempting to resume a conversation begun upstairs that morning. Liquid glugged to the surface of the flask and sat just below the rim like an old penny. He screwed on the top and stood under the arch, looking through to the conservatory he'd built on to the house for her last year.

'She is your daughter,' he said after a while.

'Yeah, yeah.'

Linda was sitting, legs apart, forearms and hands matched precisely to the arms of the padded cane chair. Her head was laid back at an angle, two pieces of cucumber in place of eyes. She sighed heavily. 'Will you leave it.'

That tone of voice. He focused for a minute on the minuscule straps of her gold sandals, her rhubarb-coloured nails. It was on the tip of his tongue to say something about example.

Wendy was sixteen. Although she wasn't Phil's, when he and Linda got married Wendy had taken his name, Fuller. Wendy was five when they first got together, young enough if she'd felt like it to call him Dad, though she never did. It had been hard: Phil had no experience of children.

'Do as your mother says,' he'd told her one bedtime, like his own father used to. But he wasn't fooling anyone; the words in his mouth lacked conviction. Wendy would take her chance, kick and scream, writhing on the floor until Linda dragged her step by step – clinging on to the banisters as if she were drowning – all the way up the stairs. Mostly Phil kept out of it.

But Wendy was growing up fast. He had to be more wary round the house, and self-consciousness made him clumsy, catching her off guard in the bathroom wearing her silvery bra, the shadow of a nipple. 'Phi-il!' she said. 'You *knew* I was in there.'

'Sorry. Sorry,' he'd say, holding up his hands.

'I hate her sometimes,' Linda said, twisting herself into the chair like a stubbed-out cigarette.

And Wendy would shout at her from the stairs, 'You bitch, you liar!'

It cut him up, that sort of language.

'I'm off, then,' he said to Linda, clutching the Thermos to his chest.

Linda grunted, arching her back, joggling the cushion to get more comfortable.

'Yeah,' she said absent-mindedly, as if his coming or going meant as little to her as the flip of the cat flap.

Someone had written CLEAN ME in the dusty black of the windows of the van, and I WISH MY WIFE WAS

THIS DIRTY. Phil climbed into the cab. It smelt of apple core and soggy cardboard. He slammed the door and put his lunch next to him on the passenger seat.

After he and Linda were married he'd decided to go into business on his own. He'd bought the van on HP, chosen a dark blue italic typeface: *Philip Fuller. Building Contractor. Buckleigh 89674*. His name in lights, he'd joked, when he brought it home and parked it for her to see on the drive. Linda'd been soft as putty then, whooping in the kitchen, coming up behind him to loop her arms around his shoulders.

'Who said size doesn't matter?' she said.

As far as Linda was concerned, this last week, he'd had a fencing job outside Barnstaple. Today Phil headed out of town, but instead of following the road north, he turned off right towards the village where he'd grown up – Bradcott – taking the road out to the disused airfield, a mile beyond the old Nissen huts. It was a place where he'd come as a boy to race cars; no doubt boys still did. It was flat and derelict, the tarmac scabby and pitted. Where the road began to dip, twisting off through trees, he touched the brake, pulling in at a familiar gateway, tucked discreetly between one bend and the next.

He sat for a moment with the engine running, then cut the ignition. Something must have been burning inside the fan – hair or fur. He wound down the window. A plastic sheep stuck to the dashboard nodded at him. Its fleece was grimy, its eyes forlorn. The sign beneath its hoof read: 'I

Love Ewe'. Linda had given it to him in the days when she used to sashay up to him holding her skirts, wearing those pink high heels, standing like a flamingo in the middle of the kitchen.

His mouth was gravel: cereal, whisky and toothpaste congealed. He unscrewed the Thermos and tipped back lukewarm coffee. It made him want to retch. He gave up the idea of rationing himself and drew from his breast pocket his silver hip flask. She'd had it engraved with his name *Phil*, and *Rock on 2000, Linda*. He stroked the serrations of metal with his thumb, and drank again, this time the burning liquid hitting the weak spot right behind his eyes.

She loved giving, she used to say, just as much as she loved receiving. She never forgot a Valentine's Day, Father's Day, anniversaries, birthdays. *Dead thoughtful* was how Frankie, her best friend, would have described her.

Phil had a collection of the cards she'd given him over the years in a shoebox on top of the wardrobe. There were evenings when she was out, he'd rummage through. *Yours for ever and ever, I love you more each day, thinking of you now and always*. Sometimes she'd sign them Linda – the dot of the 'i' drawn like a child's face – sometimes 'L', sometimes 'X'. He'd sit on the bed with them ranged like scraps of material, trying to recreate a picture of how things had been: her heat and her sparky eyes. And then he tried to pinpoint when it had happened: the twist of the rod that had brought the blinds firmly down.

He told her he'd never been good at talking. When he

tried nowadays, she'd shrug him off. 'You're beautiful, you know,' he'd say, and she'd laugh because it didn't matter to her any more. 'You are.'

Phil was staring at a pattern in the dusty foliage, a banner of torn plastic sheeting that had woven itself into the hedge. He wiped his lips, belching.

Yes, Wendy had been difficult, but she'd come round eventually, and Linda had been grateful for that. 'You're a real dad to her – more than that toe-rag of a father – what's he ever done for her?'

When Wendy was little and tucked up in bed, he and Linda had their evenings together, sitting watching TV, fish and chips on their knees. He thought they couldn't be happier.

Now Wendy stayed up late and most nights Linda had something on – yoga, dance-fitness, Frankie's.

'Can't you two find a hobby?' she'd said irritably to them. 'You could do something sporty – or join the band?'

Phil had snorted. 'I can't even hold a tune.'

'I don't know,' she said, 'anything. I don't mean "join the band", I mean get out more, have a chat, a drink.'

He'd always said he'd look after her, and he meant it. That was what marriage was about. A married woman shouldn't have to work. But although they could manage perfectly well on what he was bringing in, Linda had insisted on getting herself a job. Frankie worked in the Co-op and they were looking for part-time help. It was something to get her out of the house, Linda said, stop her going mad, give her some pocket money. It was no use arguing.

He was stubborn about it, old-fashioned.

'The money's not the point,' she'd almost scream at him. 'Face it, you want me where you can see me, stuck in the house like a doormat . . .'

Linda and Frankie used to go out to Bideford, a new club they'd discovered up there, a DJ with whom they were on first-name terms. Some nights they'd come back at two or three in the morning, giggling and blundering about in the hallway. Once he'd heard someone throwing up in the downstairs cloakroom and the next morning found Frankie, mouth agape, sprawled under the spare duvet on the settee, her perfectly honed leg, her jewel-like toes. He couldn't help wondering what it would be like waking up next to her.

'Aren't you getting a bit old for that sort of thing?' Phil might say, when eventually Linda would surface. She'd adjust her eyes witheringly.

'You'll be bumping into Wendy and her mates before you know it.'

'Eighteen, you've got to be,' she'd say, 'and you're as young as you look, thank you. We're not all gagging to draw our pensions.'

Although she'd not had sex with him for months, he still felt about her the way he'd felt when he first saw her clearing tables in the pub – as if he could follow her blindly all day. That blown-open feeling when she showed him her tongue, her melting eyes. When she'd come to sit on his knee one quiz night, he thought he'd explode with the precious weight of her, the way she giggled air, lowering her voice into his ear, her little foot broken free of its sandal.

She knew enough about men to have worked out his wiring. It was what he had found irresistible in her; and it was what drove him nowadays to despair. How easily she could get what she wanted.

When they met, Linda had made the first move, wondering, she said, how you built a house. Phil was working for Marshall's then on the new estate, and, to keep her interest, he'd offered illicitly to show her round the site. They'd had more than a few drinks by then and gone out, after ten, under a full moon. He'd made her wear a hard hat way too big from the site hut. It was like a film set: white light and exaggerated shadows that turned them into giants. She'd been holding on to him like a child, clutching his arm in delight as they paced out one of the houses at the end: the lounge, the kitchen, the cloakroom, the utility.

'If you want it, it's yours,' he'd said, swollen with bravado and the gentle pull of her on his arm. After they were married he'd added the conservatory, and over the years changed the kitchen units for her, the bathroom upstairs. He wanted to be able to buy her what she wanted – he told her that – and to watch the way her face softened when he came in at the door saying he had something for her.

'Dave's buying Frankie a Mazda for her fortieth,' she said pointedly.

'Where'd he find that kind of money?' Phil asked.

The cabin of the van darkened, as if someone had slipped a lens across the sky. Rain came on suddenly, dashing down, pinking the roof. Phil looked at himself in the slant of the mirror. The drops that hit the van echoed in the pit of his stomach. 'Listen to the rhythm of the falling rain', a song he remembered from years ago on an old jukebox. How'd it go? 'Telling me just what a fool I've been.'

Frankie and Dave had come down from Bournemouth a year ago, and Linda and Frankie had become fast friends. Hardly a day would go by, it seemed, when they weren't on the phone. The two of them fed off each other; Frankie brought round catalogues to pore over; their twin tight scooped tops, the diamanté pattern picked out on the back pockets of their jeans.

One time they'd come back from Bideford, Linda still reeking of tequila. She'd told him the sound of the buzzing in the parlour made her faint, the needle like a hundred bee stings under her skin. She'd lifted her shirt gingerly to show him – 'What's it look like?' – a livid bird with a ring in its mouth on the tip of her shoulder blade: a good excuse, for weeks, not to let him touch her.

Although it piqued him that Linda made more effort for Frankie than she did for him, he went along with the idea of the foursome. And it had seemed natural at the time – since Dave was in the trade and Phil mentioned he was looking for help – that the two of them might work together.

When it started to come out – what Dave had been up to – Linda had blamed Phil. How could he have been so stupid? How could he not have noticed? Phil was doing a stock check for the VAT return and there was a list of things missing long as your arm: posts, paint, hand tools. He felt a prickle of heat rise through his scalp like water through a rose.

How many times had Frankie and Dave been round to them for drinks, meals? Him in his rugby shirt, shaking Phil's hand at the door – his big, soft hands.

'It was you introduced me,' Phil said to Linda morosely.

'Don't lay that on me. You're the builder. What do I know? You worked with him.'

But it was Linda who got straight on the phone to Dave.

'Don't believe a word,' she said, slamming down the receiver. And when Frankie rang her back all apologetic that evening, for the first time Phil watched, almost with relief, how frosty Linda could be with someone else.

'Did you know? Did you know about this?' she said, doodling a spiky star on the pad next to the phone.

Phil could picture Frankie on her end turning on the spit of herself. *Give me one good reason*, Linda was saying.

When she came off the phone she was subdued. 'Nothing to do with Frankie,' she shrugged. 'She didn't know nothing.'

'He's her husband.'

'Doesn't mean nothing,' Linda said.

'Well, what's she going to do?'

'She's going to talk to him. See what's been going on.'

Phil sat down heavily. 'Listen,' he said. He sighed and clasped his hands behind his neck so that he was looking at her along the sights of his forearms. He was smiling oddly. 'We can't carry on like this.'

He brought his elbows down and crossed his arms around his body. 'I'm just saying.'

He'd been asleep; he woke with his face pressed yellow against the glass, drooling. He sat up straight and shunted his jaw. It had stopped raining, although above him the cloud was low-lying and oppressive. He watched where a magpie was furtively pecking at something crimson and grey, flattened to the tarmac. It was nearly five. He started the engine, an insult to the quiet and to his head, and then in fits and starts he drove away, so stiff, it felt as if his limbs had been set in plaster.

At home the garage was open, and he parked. He sat for a while in the oily light, breathing creosote and sawdust. Then he pulled out the keys and tossed them in front of his eyes, snatched them from the air, rallying himself. He was whistling grimly between his teeth some song Wendy played over and over, 'You're Beautiful'. But he was stopped short as soon as he got inside the door to the utility. Linda was there waiting for him, triumphantly waving a white stick of something under his nose.

'Guess where I found this?'

I hate you. I hate you. I hate you, he heard sobbing from upstairs.

Phil couldn't focus. He was thinking, *sweets*, then, *drugs* . . . Linda was hopping around so that he couldn't move.

'And look, look!' She was pointing at a tiny window in the plastic, a faint line of blue.

'Pregnant. That's what that means. It was in her bag, in

her bedroom. She's been lying. They've been doing it for months. Obviously. They went off camping, that time – months ago. "With Sarah", she said, do you remember? My foot. I saw Sarah's mother today – she knew nothing about it. Made me look a right fool.'

Phil let the anorak fall from his shoulders. He turned to hang it up.

'She's not listening to a word I say,' Linda said. 'You try. See if you can knock some sense into her.'

He was flinching, almost level with her mouth, backed against the ironing board.

There was a permanent DO NOT DISTURB Blu-tacked to Wendy's bedroom door, a red sticker from the Highway Code: NO ENTRY, and a poster, torn where it snagged around the handle, of thirteen different kinds of pony.

Phil knocked. 'Can I come in?'

There was no response. He pushed and sloped in around the door.

'All right?'

Wendy was on the bed, hugging her knees. She shuddered. He smelt tobacco but ignored it.

He sidled around a heap of dirty clothes and came to sit on the edge of the bed, leaned forward clasping his hands.

'She's your mother, you know. She cares about you.'

Wendy snorted and a clear glob of snot dangled over her lips.

'She wants what's best for you – come on. You know she does.'

For a minute neither of them spoke. Then Wendy wiped her nose and pulled a pillow against her tummy. Her cheeks were flushed, mascara had bled to leave a tiny row of dots under each eye. She was sullen. *He's not my dad*, she used to sob, *he's not my dad. I don't have to do what he says.*

Her skin was mottled right up to her neck as if crying had infected her all over.

Phil took a breath. 'Your mum's told me,' he said, 'about the camping. You shouldn't have lied, you know. We need to know where you are.'

'It was ages ago. She'd never have let me.'

He shifted on his seat.

She said, 'It's got nothing to do with it, anyway. She's obsessed with camping: nothing happened.'

'Well, camping aside –' he said, struggling to keep on the right side of her, 'I'm glad you had a good time. I'm sure your mum is too.'

'She doesn't care what I do. She doesn't give a shit.'

'You know that's not right,' Phil said.

'Anyway,' she looked at him directly. 'It doesn't matter now. I love him,' she said, as if these were her final words on the subject, 'and he loves me.'

For a moment Phil was winded. She was resting her head on her kneecaps, drawing herself in like a cocoon. He watched as if she were on the other side of a fence, unreachable – his hands could only lock on the metal mesh. She was so sure of herself, contained in a blue-green haze that made sand of his bones.

* * *

When he got downstairs Linda had the lights turned low and a film on. He recognised the music. She had a box of tissues beside her. He poured himself a drink, sat at the kitchen table, playing disconsolately with a round, cork place mat.

'Don't know how you can sit and watch it all through again,' he said.

Linda pulled her knees up on to the settee and tucked her legs under.

After a while he asked, 'Do you want to know what she said?'

Linda didn't move. 'She can do what she likes.'

'You don't mean that.'

'What can I do?' She turned her head, without looking at him. 'I might have known you'd be no use, backing me up.'

Phil tried to spin the mat like a huge coin. 'She says she loves him.'

'You what?' Linda darted a look over her shoulder. 'Don't make me laugh.'

'Don't you remember how it felt, at that age?'

'As a matter of fact. No.'

His voice came out unexpectedly light. 'That's about the size of it, then.' He placed the mat on the very edge of the table and flipped it in a somersault.

However many times Linda watched it, the film always made her cry. She went into a trance, reaching for the crisps in the bowl on the arm of the sofa, feeding her mouth automatically. He'd sat through it with her once to see the special effects – not all they were cracked up to be: the way the iceberg made a crunch like car wheels on gravel. He used to put his arm round her when she cried in a film. Nowadays she'd bat him off: the crying was between the screen and her, a kind of bloodletting.

He was balancing the mat upright on the table, counting the seconds he could get it to stand still. He wasn't going to say anything until the end: the freezing bit, all those faces trying to hold their noses above water; and then watching, as the camera dipped under, the hundreds of legs treading a slow dance, and belongings – a gold watch, a coin, a doll – spiralling away through an element that was thickening, fast as the air in his chest, to jelly.

RICHARD

He'd brought it home, into the front room; fumbled for the low-slung coffee table and laid it down. Then he went back to the doorway to switch on the light. The room was cold; it smelt of his mother, rose water and violet creams, but also of something sharper, stirring as he moved through the room: the damp, earthy scent of his groin.

His mother would be asleep by now. Richard called up to her from the hallway: no sign. To take the edge off the room, he turned on the fire. Then, because he felt the need to put the brakes on, he sat back, still in his overcoat, flat against the bosom of the settee, looking at the box on the table, as if it were a child's theatre poised to reveal the story of how it came to be there, landed in his lap like a gift from the gods.

On Wednesdays he'd finish his shift at half three. Usually he'd pick up a paper from the Cabin and come straight back home, have a kip. They'd have their tea together in the kitchen, macaroni cheese and Battenberg, and then he'd let her sit and watch *Countdown*.

Later he'd go out for a drink, just like his father used to; it was a way of reassuring her that he was getting on with his life, that she wasn't holding him back. He'd throw her names, tell her what so-and-so was up to.

For some time, he'd looked forward to Wednesdays. It was band night, and after practice a dozen or so of the players, including Julie, would end up in the Red Lion. Richard would get there before any of them arrived, perched like a man on stilts on a high stool by the bar, well into his third pint by the time they all turned up. Shelley would be on her own behind the bar until Nigel got there. She had to cope for the less busy part of Wednesday and Friday evenings, until he got in from rehearsals to give her a hand.

She'd been stuck on her own this evening with Richard, watching his beer go down like bathwater, turning a cloth round in a dilatory way on an ashtray or a glass. She'd learned to avoid getting into conversation with him and as soon as Nigel turned up, let Nigel serve him.

There was a core of them who always appeared about nine and the names came flooding back to Richard. There were the older ones, Stan from the garage, Bill Scott – practically dead – and then his own generation, Robert Woodward, Jimmy Falk – they'd hardly changed since school, when he'd been 'lamp post', 'beanpole' – and although he'd never been part of their gang, they nodded to him if they passed him in the street, or met him at the door with their mail, patronising. 'Thanks, postie.'

Richard had been determined to get out of Buckleigh as soon as he could. At seventeen he'd joined the navy, a merchant seaman for another fifteen years, and then made a bit of cash out on the oil rigs. He'd come back recently, after his dad died. With none but personal references (and those secured by his mother), he was lucky to have got the job.

It was in the band crowd he'd first spotted Julie. Julie Westaway. He'd known her three sisters by sight (all married now) but she'd been a late baby, an afterthought, still in a pram when the last of them was leaving seniors. Julie wasn't like the others, not even her father or mother. There was something clean and untouched about her, the first, precious flower of the season.

And she was laughing now, next to her fatter, brown-haired friend, as if, from where she was sitting, a tide had been turned. She was clearly enjoying being the centre of attention, wiping her cheeks, blowing her nose.

'Don't mind 'im. Don't know what 'e'm talkin' 'bout,' Bill, the ancient and huge euphonium player was saying, cajoling her.

And another, 'Does the same to little boys, right on stage – middle of a contest – has a go. For one wrong note. He should wrap it up better, but he don't – be more careful what he says. He'll not have anyone left to shout at if he doesn't mind out.'

'Never mind,' said Julie, 'I'm all right now. Silly.'

'You shouldn't have to put up with it. None of us should. One of these days –' Robert said, who had plans of his own for the band.

'He's just like it,' she said, smoothing down her skirt, placatory. 'It's his band. I don't suppose he'll change.'

'He needs to get a life,' the dark girl said, 'he's obsessed.'

Richard had perfected the art of listening while looking

deep in thought. He'd take in the band and her shining face under the guise of a broad sweep of the lounge – the dartboard, the photo of the landlord's dogs, whoever was in the alcove table (a silent, wistful couple usually), and then the long table of the snug, which the band, sometimes still in their purple and gold uniforms, liked to appropriate.

'How's it going?' he asked Nigel, who lifted the drawbridge of the bar to let himself in.

'Good,' Nigel said. 'Bit of a bashing from Wheeler this evening,' he nodded towards Julie, 'but we've contests to do. Tense time of year.'

'What do you play, then?'

'Trombone.'

'What, the hairpin thing?' Richard curled his fist around his mouth and worked his other hand like a lever.

Nigel humoured him. 'Yep. Coolest one.'

'Few girls you got there – when d'you let them in?'

'Always been mixed, long as I've been around.'

'Recognise that one,' Richard said, lifting his head, 'knew her sister: Westaway, Sharon.'

Richard was fishing. He already knew her name from the birthday cards he'd delivered to the house in April.

'Julie. She's a good little player.'

'Got the mouth for it.'

Nigel's lips were plump like a girl's. He had a colourless oval face, as if he didn't get out in the light much.

Julie had been drinking rum and Coke. It was near closing and she made a move to stand but lost her balance, slipped back down. Her friend was shrieking with laughter, but it was enough to get them all looking at their watches, knocking back chairs. They made a song and dance of saying goodbye, take care, two of them still snuffling round the girls. They couldn't do enough, helping them on with their jackets and to the door, Robert offering to walk someone home, another crying out, 'Watch the road!' and winking.

Ten minutes later, when the bar was back to gloom, Shelley went over to wipe the table and collect the last of the empties. She must have stubbed her toe on something because she stopped and bent to peer between the table legs, pulling out a dark, bulky object.

'Look what they've left behind!'

Nigel was putting chairs up on tables; he came over.

'Cornet,' he said. 'Bet that's Julie's. She was in a right state tonight.'

Richard raised his hand from where he was sitting. 'What's that?'

'Instrument,' Nigel said. 'Never mind, I'll take it for her.'

Richard unhitched himself from the stool and came across, standing too close. Shelley was crouching down. She shuffled before she got up so that she'd be at a remove from him, laying the case gently on the table. There was a round white label stuck to the lid, its black type formal, *Trevada Music, Cambourne*, and then, below, following the line of the circle in jagged biro, *J. Westaway. Bondstones*.

'Julie. Told you,' Nigel said. 'She'd forget her head if it wasn't stitched on.'

'I can take it if you like – drop it off on the round

tomorrow,' Richard said, holding out his hand, surprising himself by the way a plan had so quickly blossomed in his head. 'She'd get it first thing then, before she misses it.'

Shelley looked at him and he could see her hesitate. 'You sure?' She was clutching it still, looking at Nigel, who shrugged. Richard began to worry that he'd have to do or say something rash to persuade her.

'No trouble to me,' he said.

She let it go. 'OK then, good of you.'

'Only me!' he'd called up, and there'd been no reply. Once his mother was asleep, she was generally dead to the world. He'd been holding the rigid handle of the case so tightly that pink lines had impressed themselves to his palm. He steadied his nerve now by running his hands over its battered edges, the frayed whiskers of thread.

The clasps in front of him were dull silver and geometrically patterned – they reminded him of his father's cigarette case, never used, but kept in a drawer as if it were precious. Richard gathered his coat around him and knelt down, shuffled back on his haunches to be nearer the fire, and then reached out to flick the catches. They shot up, alarming as pheasants from the undergrowth.

It crossed his mind that the case might not contain an instrument after all, but other things, embarrassing women's things, tankloads of the potions and creams they put on their faces. He cocked his ear to the ceiling to check again that all was quiet upstairs, and then he lifted the lid.

The instrument shone out from the box like her blonde

hair. Like treasure curled up. He thought of the angel in church, high up, arched against a truss of the roof, her wormy cheeks blowing, and he compared them to Julie's, peaches and cream. Julie was *more* of an angel. Lying there in plum-coloured plush, the back row of a cinema.

He reached out and touched, the pads of his fingers stuck where they came into contact with the stickiness of ice. He cupped his hands under and lifted the cornet shyly as if it were a puppy or a kitten, afraid of dropping it, of inadvertently breaking a limb in his clumsiness, all fingers and thumbs.

He took his time, turning it in his hands, inspecting the markings on it. There was a penny-sized stamp of a globe containing a B and an H, a stave wafting behind like a Hollywood scarf, trailing wild musical notes. And then – he almost cried out loud – just below it, a tiny capital R with a circle around it, his own name, a sudden rush of affirmation that brought the world to his feet – everywhere he'd ever been: hot sand, monsoon, ocean, the hooting of ports. As though he'd made an instant loop of the earth, the colour of the room confirming it: the orange fire, the heady swirls of furniture, the liquid of the overhead light, even himself, as he looked straight into the cornet's flare, tipped upside down, peering round, the frame of his glasses, his eye, suddenly huge, a fish eye at a door.

The instrument was heavier than it looked and he took it firmly in both hands, shivering with pleasure at how easily he was able to find his way around. Here was a support for his little right finger – another surge of validation – a curl of metal tailor-made. He began to toy with bringing the thin blunt end towards his mouth, but as he focused on the implausibly narrow circle of the tube, he realised in a panic that there was something missing. He turned in dismay to the inside of the case, expecting to see nothing but emptiness. But, set low in the box, there was a rectangular compartment with a tag of velvet. Trembling, he lifted it. Inside, in state, lay the mouthpiece – two triumphant hoots of the ship's whistle – which he picked out, a miniature funnel of burnished metal. He brought the two pieces of silver, the smaller piece and the body of the instrument, up close, slotted them miraculously together.

Julie Westaway, curled up on his knee. Everything before him, her: the studs of metalwork that held the tubes in place just as her earrings punctured her marzipan flesh; the intimate folds and bends of her body, like a dance; the one, two, three of the valves – three steps to heaven – her buttons.

He knew what he was going to do, what he had been waiting to do since he'd first taken possession. His mouth was dry: Julie, Snow White, her rosebud lips, her little mouth for putting cherries in, here she was, his Cinderella, his princess. He lifted the instrument, brought its golden font to his lips, focusing along the sights of the cornet, fingers poised above the three top hats, and leant tentatively forward: the exquisite touch of lip on lip, the taste of rank lipstick metal, pressing where she had been. He gathered himself and whispered down the tube in two slow drawn-out breaths that sounded softly like wind down a drainpipe, hardly perceptible, 'Julie – lovely bitch.'

WATERFALL

He wasn't sure what to wear. Trainers, since they were walking. But then he wanted to look reasonably smart. He'd wear his grey trousers and a shirt. Richard looked at himself against the mirror on the wardrobe, smoothed back his hair. It was still thick at the front and he kept it short, though it was greying round his ears. Not bad for forty-five. He pulled in his stomach, puffed out the cage of his chest and clenched his interlocking hands, turning side on, straightening his back. He blew between pursed lips like a weightlifter. Could be worse, he thought. Then he crouched down and pulled the trainers out from their box under the wardrobe. They were new and white, glowing almost; he sat on the edge of the bed and worked them open, pressed his feet home, tying the thick new laces in a bow, retying them so that the two loops fell exactly equal like rabbit's ears on either side. He stood up and looked down into the well of the mirror to inspect them, worried they might make his feet look too big. And then, impatiently, he turned away.

He went over to the window and tugged at the curtain. The sun was bronze behind a grey wash of cloud that would soon burn off. He was still sweating from his bath. He wiped himself again with the pink towel and then took down the pale striped shirt, which his mother had ironed and hung on the back of his bedroom door for him.

He'd told her, eating toast, that he was going out to Lydford.

'We used to go there – you and your sister –' she'd said accusingly.

'That's why I thought of it.'

'See if it's still there?' She sniffed. 'Perhaps I'd like to go again, too?'

Richard made an effort to regulate his breathing, feeling his chest expand like metal springs. 'Well I'll check it out,' he said, 'you wouldn't get far, though, with your knees.'

She had turned her back on him. 'I could sit somewhere. Nice day out,' she was muttering.

'Let's see how I get on.'

'You taking someone, then?'

'Not sure yet,' he lied.

'All dressed up?' She twisted round with that beady look.

'No,' he looked down at himself. 'My work trousers, that's all.'

'I won't ask,' she said, turning away again, adjusting the kettle on the stove.

'I've got my mobile,' he said, 'you can always call.'

'Managed so far. On my own. Don't you worry about me. You get off.'

He couldn't be bothered to remonstrate. And he'd be

late. He pushed his plate towards the centre of the table and went upstairs to finish dressing.

Shutting the front door was like closing a fridge, the artificial light, the sense of things wilting at the edges. Richard slung his thin blue jacket over his shoulder, determined not to hear his mother if she should call him back.

As he drove down the high street, he stuck out his tongue and panted. He slowed down, twisting to fiddle with the blister-pack in his pocket, unpopping some tan-coloured chewing gum. He didn't want to be late, but he didn't want to be early either, hanging around. As he turned the corner, past the Co-op, it looked as if he'd got it just right: there, surely, was Julie, the back of her approaching the bus stop, turning towards the sound of the car like a little bird, her tiny steps.

For a moment he was aware again of his feet, which felt clumsy on the pedals. But as she turned, her face betrayed a shy dawn of recognition. She stood back a little to let him draw up.

'Hello,' he said through the half-open window, leaning over to get the handle, giving the door a shove. 'How are you? Jump in.'

Julie clutched her bag as she sat herself down. She was wearing a flowery skirt, calf length. And she had a cream blouse with a round neck, lower than she'd been wearing recently – a narrow margin of pale flesh showing between the edge of her top and the coarser skin at her throat.

'Thanks,' she said.

The car smelt of industrial pine. She wasn't sure if it was him at first, or the car. She could smell cigarettes too.

He was chewing as if he were riding a bicycle uphill. 'Trying to give up,' he said. 'You ever smoked?'

'No.'

'Don't start. Nasty habit.'

Julie was polite. 'Mum used to. But she doesn't now.'

'Second time I've tried to kick it.' His chewing intensified and she watched the gum at the front of his mouth like a sock in a drying machine.

'Right then?' He put the car in gear. 'Let's go.'

They drove out of the square. She wondered if anyone had seen them. The interior of the car was spotless, the windscreen gleaming green and pink from the inside. It was only when they'd cleared town, out on the main link road, that she dared to look beyond the window: past the cricket ground, the kennels – two young girls in green kennel T-shirts walking a clutch of dogs. She was excited and nervous: it was the first time she'd been taken out by someone she didn't really know, driven by a stranger, in a strange car. She couldn't look at his face, just his competent hand on the gearstick, its spidery hairs.

'I knew your eldest sister,' he said, glancing round quickly, 'Sharon – wonder if she'd remember?' Sharon was twenty when Julie was born.

'Were you at the college?' Julie asked, surprised.

'A few years ago now.' He grunted and she realised when she met his eyes briefly, full on, that this was how he laughed.

'She used to hang around with older boys,' he said.

'Sharon didn't like school. She didn't like the Head.'

'Him! Basket case. Nutter. Quite right. Where did you go?'

'Community College, the same. But it was Mrs Trotter then. I left in the sixth form – halfway through. I'm with the bank. Barclays. They take you on. Train you.'

'Here?'

'No. You start in the big branch. Okehampton.'

She was putting down the tiniest roots, relaxing into the car seat. He wasn't too hard to talk to. She hadn't been able to picture his face and Tracey had made her doubt herself, saying he was old enough to be her father, but he wasn't bad-looking – much better-looking than her dad, anyway – and not fat or saggy.

'It's nice to get out,' she said, pleased with what she could now identify as her capacity for small talk. A year ago, before the bank, she'd have been at sea.

'Good. That's what I thought.' He hunched forward over the steering wheel as he negotiated the two mini round-abouts, on to the ring road and over to the other side of the A30. He was concentrating on driving. She supposed he'd have to be a good driver, being a postman. He drove smoothly. The engine purred softly. She turned up her toes, which she'd painted red, then clenched them back under cover of the strap. Perhaps she should have chosen some-thing less obvious?

She had tucked her hands under her thighs.

'Thanks again for bringing my cornet back,' resuming the conversation they'd had last week. He thought again of how he'd almost missed his chance, how he'd had to pluck himself from walking down the cinder path and straight out through the garden gate, turning as he took hold of the cold iron-work and blurting, 'Don't suppose you'd fancy going out somewhere?'

He'd suspected it might have been a ruse, the 'don't-ring-me-I'll-ring-you' routine; and then, that he should have given her his mobile number, but he wasn't certain in his fluster that he'd remember it correctly. Anyway, she had rung, and he'd managed to get to the phone before his mother. So far, it had been easy, miraculously easy. She was there, where she said she'd be, and she'd climbed in, quite chatty. He realised it was up to him to keep momentum going.

'Been in the band long?'

'Since I was about ten.'

'You must be good.'

'Not really,' she said, though she was pleased. She was good. She was in the front row.

'I'll have to listen out for you next time. They had a band on ship – made you feel like you belonged to something when they played.'

She looked at him in profile: his purplish chin, the skin where it was stretched almost translucent over his cheeks. There was a sprig of moisture on his upper lip.

'I'd like to travel one day,' she said. 'America maybe. Or Australia.'

'One place I've never been. Like the sound of it.'

'I've a friend got relatives there. Christmas on the beach.'

They had turned off the main road. It seemed more sheltered here; the may trees were in blossom: a cherry, a magnolia flaring in a front garden. They passed through a village, a pub, a cul-de-sac of squat council houses, and then a row of stone cottages, their wicket gates.

'Nice here, isn't it? Lovely . . .' she said, peering round.

'Yes. Quiet. Pricey.'

He flicked the indicator – its clean, respectable metronome – and pulled up in a track that crunched with newly laid gravel. There was a car park at the end boxed out with neat low hedges like an archaeological excavation. There were two other cars stationed strategically in opposite corners.

'Here we are. Lydford Gorge. Not too busy, mid-week. Lovely day for it,' he said.

When she got out of the car, she smoothed her skirt and slung her small leather bag across her shoulder, resting her hand on its pouch. She'd filled it carefully in the morning – lipstick, money and a packet of tissues from the newsagents, little pink and gold love hearts on them, all they had left.

'Got everything?' he said. She liked the confidence with which he addressed her, as if he'd known her already.

'Yes, I think so.'

'I'll grab my jacket.' He dived in and brought it out, swung it over his shoulder in the way he'd practised, by the hook of his first finger.

The sun was shining, everything around them glazed with honeyed light. It wasn't too hot; there was a slight breeze that lifted her fine hair. As they approached the smart brown wood and glass of the reception area, he caught sight of their reflections walking towards them: him and her, so real and lifelike, it was as if they might meet and swap places.

Two women in their retirement were manning the desk and had watched Julie and Richard as they approached from the driveway, Julie totting behind him in her strappy sandals which made her walk differently, a going-out walk. The women were smiling corporately as they entered the vestibule. Richard had his wallet out and raised his chin. 'Two, please.'

'Two — adults?'

There was something about the way the woman asked that raised his hackles.

'Two. Full price,' he said, refusing to meet her eye. She had proprietorial hair, rolled back stiffly from her face. Both women were wearing green-leaf National Trust headscarves around their necks. Richard handed over a note, leaning sideways and tapping his trousers. 'Hang on, I might just have the change.'

He pulled out a handful of coins, sifting it on his palm. 'There you go.' He wanted to show her that he knew about shop etiquette.

'Lovely day you've chosen,' she said, tilting her head so that she could inspect him through the lower halves of her glasses.

'Have a map,' the other one was saying, skinnier, greyer-looking. She licked her finger, lifting a leaflet from a pile in front of her, and waited for Richard's attention. She opened it out for him, leaning forward, revealing a scrawny triangle at her neck.

'You can go the long way, here, past the White Lady, or you can go the short. Not too strenuous. No heart condition?'

Richard took it from her and folded it in half. Julie smiled at them like she smiled at all old women, sympathetically, thinking about how dreadful it would be to be incontinent, and followed him out.

Richard needed to move to keep his balance. He was breathing shallowly, past the outside pen of the tea rooms, whose tables were being sprayed and rubbed down, and towards a kissing gate with a wooden sign above it like a hatstand.

'Right,' he said, looking up, 'your choice.'

Julie too felt light-headed. Partly it was the shoes: as if she were following him late at night, outside a nightclub, back to the car. She looked up and read the sign dutifully but it made no sense to her. Ahead of them was a family, the father poring over a large wooden diagram, tracing, for the benefit of his wife, the black line of the various paths. She was clearly distracted by the two or three young children who were batting about them excitedly.

The man turned from the map, exasperated. 'Concentrate,' he said. 'Do what we say. Keep to the path and if you're good, we'll have ice cream.' The children made a noise like geese.

'Calm down. Let's be sensible,' the man said. 'We've got a lot of walking first.'

"Scuse,' Richard said, taking the lead and weaving his way between them; Julie followed. When they were on their own he said, 'Didn't want to be stuck behind that lot, screaming kids. All right to go the long way?' looking at her shoes. 'Doubt there'll be much mud today?'

Julie nodded, not wanting to appear like a girl who couldn't accept a challenge, but she could already feel the thin black straps beginning to rub where they circled her ankles.

Richard was relieved to be among trees, clenching and unclenching his fists, watching the way the skinny trunks braced themselves against the increasingly vertiginous angle of the drop. It wasn't long before the path narrowed. They were beginning to climb upwards and he motioned decorously for Julie to go first. He wanted to see her from behind, the way she moved her hips, swaying from one side to the other under the extraordinary bustle of her skirt. The skin on her ankles was pale, a nimbus of blonde hair as she lifted her feet. He wanted to catch the female scent of her. He'd have liked an excuse to push her from behind, sink his hands into her buttocks, which despite the rest of her slight frame had all the bearing and roll of a working animal. She leant forward and by leaning seemed to offer herself up to him.

'Steep this bit,' he said, breathing out in a whistle.

Halfway up there was a bench and sitting on it, to his dismay, a couple of pensioners, him wheezing, mopping his brow with a handkerchief, her primly next to him in a lemon Aertex shirt.

'Morning,' Julie sang to them under her breath.

The man raised and dropped his arm limply. 'Lovely day,' he said, deadpan.

The air around the couple smelt of soap flakes. Richard kept Julie going, walking closely behind her for a hundred yards or so, until they reached the top of the climb and another bench.

'I'm so unfit,' she said, clapping her sides. She brushed a space on the roughly made seat, and sat down, blinking as if taking in the view for the first time.

'Wow. Look at that!'

The gorge fell steeply beneath their feet and reared up on the other side, prickly with trees. There was a sliver of water running in and out along the bottom like a stitch. 'We'll get down there in a bit,' Richard said, a bead of sweat rolling towards his eye.

'Should have brought a camera,' she said, 'it's lovely up here.'

It touched him like a wire, that she should want a record of this moment. He was exhilarated, intensely aware of the warm thermals of her breath. The gorge plunged in a way that invited him to rush at her, to roll with her down like a pinball between the light grey trunks of trees, each knock an emerald or a purple glow that would light up the leaves as they descended. He looked at her and his mouth, which had been dry, watered. He could have sucked himself up into her skirts, head squashed between her thighs, suffocated –

He'd sat down next to her, a hand's width between them.

'I used to come here with my sister.'

'What does she do?' Julie asked.

'Marianne? Married. Lives in Northampton. Two kids.'

'You're an uncle?'

'We don't really get on, me and my sister.'

'Boys or girls?' Julie persisted.

'Girls.'

Julie wanted babies. To cuddle them. 'I love children.' She looked at him sideways.

Richard was thinking about the time he'd been caught out by his mother. She'd gone to see what was wrong with Marianne in the room next door to his, sobbing, fighting off the bedclothes, saying she couldn't breathe. When their mother had eventually managed to calm her down, promising to leave both landing lights on, she'd come to check on Richard and found him sitting bolt upright on the edge of his bed.

'What're you doing still up?'

'Couldn't sleep.'

'Did Marianne wake you?'

'She was making a noise.'

His mother had sat down next to him, making the bed slump and him fall against her. In those days her hair was brown and smelt of furniture polish. She was the only one he'd let touch him. She bent her head to his ear and said soothingly, 'Have you been in Marianne's bedroom?'

It wasn't to do with stealing or drawing rude words on a wall, just a pillow to shut her up: there seemed no reason not to tell her. 'I wanted to stop the noise . . .'

The way she had looked at him, drawing back, not hugging

144

him, her eyes getting tight and sorry, he'd known that she wouldn't keep it to herself – she'd blab to Dad sooner or later.

'Do you?' Julie said shyly.

Richard looked nonplussed.

'. . . like children?'

He made himself pause as if to consider the question. 'Haven't really thought about it – bit noisy for my liking.'

As if on cue there were yelps and whoops rising from the path below them and two boys emerged chasing each other, veering to and from the edge of the gorge. A deep grating voice pursued them. 'Charlie – don't!'

The children took no notice and continued to wheel about, firing at each other as they came past Richard and Julie with pointed fingers.

'Stop there. This minute. Wait!' The voice loomed into view: the man who'd been poring over the map, his forearms extended like shafts of a cart. The boys, all knees and elbows, had already disappeared. The man stopped just short of the bench, bent down and rested his hands on his thighs, exhaling precise, sporty breaths. He was wearing long khaki shorts with flapped pockets on the outside, chunky sandals that revealed big muscular toes. He turned round to wait for his wife; she was blotchy-faced and anxious, dragging a little blonde-haired girl after her. For a few seconds he trod the ground, then, motioning back to her with a jerk of his head, he set off again calling, 'Charlie! Mikey!'

When she reached them, the wife was whispering mechanically, 'Good girl, stay with Mummy, we'll catch those naughty boys, won't we. Naughty boys.' She didn't lift her head to acknowledge Richard or Julie, as if she could see, by the way they were sitting, that they were involved in something that might be a little sordid or inappropriate.

Richard sat with his legs apart, feeling the sun penetrate the dense weave of his trousers. His thighs were beginning to sweat.

She was wondering whether she should ask him. She'd nearly said it in the car, to make conversation. She tried it out in her head. And then when he looked round at her as if he wanted her to say something, she blurted, 'Do your friends still call you Beanpole?'

Where'd she got that from? For a second he wobbled. *Was she laughing at him?* He was flustered, as if she'd touched bare flesh.

'Someone said that's what they called you, someone in the band, when you were at school.'

He bit the inside of his lip and looked at her sharply. Her face changed – a tide of regret, as if a hand had passed over it.

'I'm tall, you see.'

'Sorry if—'

'Six foot two. What about you?' he said, recovering himself. 'Any nicknames?'

'Not really,' she said. 'Sisters call you names – because I was the baby. Not nice ones though.'

'They called me Rick in the navy.'

She smiled. 'Rick. It suits you.'

He closed his legs, then crossed them uneasily. But

movement only further encouraged what had been an involuntary twitch, releasing a pulse into his bloodstream, a rush he felt to the tips of his ears, too late to stifle. He got to his feet. 'Better keep moving,' he said. 'The oldies'll catch us up else.'

He jigged behind her for a bit, surreptitiously adjusting himself, and then he caught up where the path widened. 'Do you like music? Apart from band stuff, I mean?'

'Yes, all sorts – dance, disco and that.'

'I suppose I'm a bit out of touch. Used to listen to it, played things full blast in my room. The Who, bands like that – before your time I expect?'

Julie looked at him blankly.

'It all sounds the same to me now – there's nothing new – all been done before.'

'I like Coldplay,' she said shyly.

He shrugged. 'I'm not a complete dinosaur. I like my computer – surfing the Net. That's a hobby of mine.'

'Good for shopping,' she said.

'You can find out all sorts of things now, things people don't want you to find out. Unbelievable things. Like – say – 9/11.'

He paused for emphasis, but she was oblivious, tripping alongside, trying to keep up. He carried on more excitedly, 'We take so much for granted. We believe what we're told. But that sort of thing, they can't keep it from us any more. It's public knowledge. We're not as stupid as they think. We ask questions. And you get the answers, there's all sorts of experts spelling it out –'

Julie was making a show of listening, but this was man's talk and she was happy to let it flow over her head.

'Inside job. That's the bottom line. Those people on the plane: dead meat. The price they paid for getting into Iran. Take the Pentagon –'

Julie nodded because he seemed to require it.

'Well, how come there was no wreckage? A plane – a Boeing 757 – a plane like that would've been scattered for miles. Fuel tanks alone, blown the place sky-high. So how come it came down clean as a whistle? No mess on the ground?'

'I'm not very good with politics,' Julie said. 'It's depressing, Mum says, they never give the good news.'

They were walking down a narrow path, enclosed on either side by steep beech hedges. Halfway along they were aware of a rushing sound so loud it could have been an army plane, low-flying off the moor, but the sky above was clear as an egg. They emerged to a small wooden bridge across a narrow stretch of river which, as they stepped on to it, seemed to vibrate. On the other side, a broad pool opened up on to a pebbly beach, and from high above, careering down into the surface like a corkscrew, there was a molten coil of water.

'Look at that,' said Julie, her mouth hanging open.

They stood side by side, marvelling at the sheer plunge of it. For a moment Richard was entranced, and then he had a niggling sense of déjà vu: the way the waterfall tore its strip from the world in an endlessly projected picture. It was an image he'd watched again and again: the silvery walls

of the World Trade Center, a bird flying to meet the archi-
tecture of its own collapse – flutter, flutter, flutter: BOUF.

He said, 'It's like a film, isn't it?'

Julie looked round at him and smiled to see his childish
delight. But then she followed his glance as, above them,
he spotted the flag of a lemon T-shirt.

'Let's keep going for now, shall we?' he said.

It was when she stopped that Julie felt the throbbing in
her feet, both heels raw at the back. She tried to put it from
her mind. They were more or less on the flat, low down as
you could be, the sun reaching through in greenish shafts.
In some parts the path was naturally formed from speckled
granite, jutting out over the river, so narrow in places that
an iron rail had been set in the rock to hold on to.

'It's like being an explorer,' Julie said.

'Slippy here,' he said. 'Careful.'

She liked the way he told her to look out, and she liked
playing the little girl, taking baby steps, wobbling, waiting
for him before she went ahead.

They kept going, the river squeezed between the
buttresses of its banks, rising so steeply they were contained
in discreet pockets all the way along. Then they emerged
to a man-made staircase, the grids of its construction
clanking under them like an old fire escape. They were led
along a series of pools, each gouged from the rock by a
drill of water so loud they couldn't hear to speak; walking
against the current, upstream, the noise and the reverse
movement of water disorienting and claustrophobic. When
they broke out above the pools it was a relief to find the

river stretched lazy and flat, room on the path for them to walk abreast.

'Does your head in after a bit, doesn't it?'

'It's amazing,' she said.

He touched her elbow and for a moment she wasn't sure what he meant by it. He was gazing intently at the glassy surface of the river.

'Watch. Can you see? Look, they're jumping.'

It was the first time he'd touched her and she felt his hand like a burn. It made her heart skip, not unpleasantly, but she wasn't sure how to react. She shifted her arm gently. And then she saw: fishes long as a finger, mouths wide open, propelling themselves into the air, stamping the surface with rings that came and went as if something invisible hopped there.

'Wow! Are they trying to breathe?' she asked, still wondering whether the touch had been deliberate.

'They're after flies,' he said. 'Come on, it gets better.'

Ahead of them the path divided: one track, marked EXIT, twisted up steeply; the other continued to follow the course of the riverbank. Walls of purple-grey rock began to close them in on either side and they clambered their way in single file until, again, they could hear children ahead, stomping up and down another metal gangway, at the head of which a white board advertised: DEVIL'S CAULDRON. MAXIMUM: 15 PERSONS ANY ONE TIME.

'They'll be gone in a minute,' Richard said. 'We'll have it to ourselves.'

The big man and his wife were coming back, approaching

them from the far end of the walkway, cajoling the little girl between them to walk just a bit further. One of her brothers pushed ahead between them, reminded of the promise of ice cream. Richard and Julie stood back to let them pass. Then they climbed up.

It was chilly out of the sun, moisture glistening on the surface of the rock. A plant clung in the crevices, whose heart-shaped, fleshy leaves were pressed like a thumb in a clavicle. All along the walkway, glinting in the river beneath their feet, was a trail of copper and silver coins. Richard remembered as a boy how desperate he'd been to climb in and make his fortune.

The rush of water began to beat again like a hammer between his ears. He was excited at the prospect of the hidden balcony: he could already see the entrance to the final cave, streaky with greens and blacks like the opening of a huge rotten mouth. But as he handed himself around the corner he was brought up short. There, interrupting the line of the rail, was the soft-limbed body of the third child, craning over towards the deep well of water.

The boy's hair was long, curling down his neck and hanging over his face. His feet were off the ground and he was balanced like a clothes peg over the barrier. Richard turned his back on him. He said hoarsely in Julie's ear, using his body to fence her from the boy, 'Do you believe in wishes?'

'Might as well,' she shouted, avoiding the intimacy of whispers, and then, gripped by the idea, grappled with the catch on her bag, pulled out a twenty-pence piece and held it up to him.

'There!' She chucked it and they watched it shudder and twist to the bottom of the river bed.

Richard pressed himself in behind her as much as he dared, pinning her to the metal, and she turned a little towards him, a question forming like a bubble between her lips. But then, suddenly, her whole face contorted and her hand lifted to meet her mouth. 'Oh my God!'

Richard, uncomprehending, stepped back from her, when everything was telling him – if only the boy would get lost – to press her home, his neck boiling, his chest; but then he realised that she was looking past him, over his shoulder and down into the swirling water. He turned distractedly to follow her gaze. Below their feet, on the surface of the pool Richard saw the white material of a T-shirt rising like petals. And then the fist of a head burst into the centre of the flower, and, from the open and shut mouth of the boy, mewlish cries began to translate themselves from the general hubbub of the cave. The boy was drumming his arms on the water, flailing at the devil who lived in there swimming in the current to meet him.

'Fuck's sake!' Richard said under his breath. Julie's face was spray-fixed and stupid-looking.

He freed himself from her and ran a few paces along the path. But there was no sign of the parents. Grimly he hung his jacket on the post of the railing and caught the top of the bar, lifted his leg over, the height of his leg, and dropped down clumsily into the icy pool. A station whistle blew in his head. The shock of it made him want to hit the boy, to knock him out. He grabbed on to him, pounding with his legs to keep his head above water, slung his arm roughly under the boy from behind. 'Come on!' he shouted at himself and at the boy. 'Come on!'

The boy's cries were weak and high-pitched. Richard fielded with his free arm and got them over to the rock side, groped his way along, thrashing with his legs until he found a handhold on the lip of the pool, kicking out to stop them both from going under. The boy had surrendered himself to Richard's grasp and was limp, his limbs lifting in the furious current. Julie was making a show of reaching out from the balcony, but was too short to be of any use.

'Get his dad,' Richard shouted up to her. 'Get him down here!'

Julie ran frantically along the metal grid. He could hear her at the end. 'Hey. Hey. Come back. Your boy. He's in the water . . .' The strain of shouting was cracking her voice.

The ice had clapped him like silver plating. He had the boy in a vice and his arm ached. 'Come on!' he shouted in the great hollow and his voice was swallowed up.

First Julie came running back, inelegantly, hands on her bag to stop it batting, and then, behind her, the man.

'Christ!' he exclaimed. 'Christ!' He leant out over the metal and reached his thick hand, motioning towards Richard in a cup-like gesture. 'Here. Hold on.'

The boy stirred himself and began to sob, twisting around, thrashing towards his father.

'Calmly, Charlie – grab on, calm now, that's it. Got you. Hold on.'

He had the boy's hand and Richard let him go with a shove. For a moment it seemed that he'd be swept away but his father had him, yellow knuckles, neck straining, every fibre of his body, and he held and pulled him up, then grasped him under his armpits and lifted him over. 'Thank God. Thank God,' he said. 'What on earth were you thinking of?'

The boy stood shivering, all bravado knocked out of him. His mother, who'd attempted to park his two siblings by the noticeboard, rushed towards him and clung to him, soaking her front, her voice shaking. 'You silly, silly boy.'

Richard had manoeuvred himself towards the balcony. He got himself half out of the water and held on tight. The weight of the pool was like tar on his back. He clung on and then with a great effort heaved himself up and, laying his weight along the bar, hoisted himself over. Julie was at his side. He wiped his nose in the crook of his arm and held his hand against his stomach, which ached as if it had been scooped out by a sharp-edged spoon.

The father turned to him. 'Thank you,' he said, 'don't know what he was doing. Appreciate your help.'

Richard shook his head and lifted his hand as if to say, *no need.*

The father said to his wife, 'Come on, let's get him back to the car. Get him dry.'

The wife had the boy around his shoulders. He was nodding uncontrollably as if his neck were on a spring, refusing to look past the end of his nose. His mother, as she ushered the boy along the path, lowered her head, cowed and apologetic.

When they were alone, Julie stroked Richard's jacket, which she had over her arm. 'He might have died!'

'He'd have managed to get out.'

'No, I don't think so. I don't think he could swim. You saved his life.'

'Oh well,' Richard said, shuddering, shrinking from her, shaking water from his fingertips. He looked down at his trainers. 'I must look ridiculous,' he said, every footstep squelching as they made their way up towards the exit.

'You did a good thing.'

'Those bloody ladies up at the top there. They'll have a laugh, won't they.'

For a moment Julie had forgotten about the old women. But then she said, 'No they won't. You rescued him. You saved him.' She sounded indignant enough, but, despite herself, the suggestion of them laughing, or trying not to laugh, entered into her head like a germ.

Out in the car park the doors of the blue Range Rover were spreadeagled and the family were loading up to go. The wife emerged, flustered from strapping in the little girl and, seeing Richard and Julie, went round to her husband's elbow. Wearily the father raised a finger to shush her, then he began to tap irritably at his pockets and set out across the gravel, looking from left to right, to head them off.

'Thanks again,' he called out awkwardly, approaching Richard for a handshake, having secreted a note to the flat of his hand with his thumb. 'Thanks.' He attempted an exchange as he took Richard's hand in his. Richard could feel the softness of the note.

'Get yourself a drink.'

Without looking, Richard put the note straight into his wet trouser pocket.

'No problem,' he said.

When they got to the car and he'd unlocked the doors, Richard stood for a moment looking in at the seat and at himself. He wasn't going to mess up the upholstery.

'You get in,' he said to Julie. 'I'll see if there's something in the back.'

He went round to the boot and lifted the lid on the warm loaf of air inside. Underneath a heavy black sports bag there was a hank of orange baling twine, a checked blanket, and a large square package of plastic sheeting. He fished the plastic out and shook it – a body's length – bringing it round to the front and arranging it carefully over the seat, tucking it into the crease at the base as if he were making a bed.

'That's lucky,' she said.

He sat down heavily and rivulets of water gathered in an outline around his thighs, finding natural channels where the material crumpled, spilling over the side. His trousers clung to him. He could smell the months of deliveries rising from them.

For a moment he bent forward, doing nothing. Then he leaned to one side and brought out the crumpled note from his pocket, smoothed it against the steering wheel.

'A fiver. Wow. His precious son's worth a fiver. Bit of an insult, don't you think?' he said.

'You must be freezing?'

'Stingy git.'

It was as if he'd slapped her. She knew at that moment what she'd tell Tracey. He went a bit weird. We didn't *do* anything . . . How all he seemed to care about was the money. *And what if he rings me? I can't. What am I going to say?*

It was a stupid place to come. What was he thinking? All those people around. He had wanted so much to touch her hair, to see how it felt, falling down with her, but he'd lost his appetite. There was something too humiliating about the way he was being looked at, leaking all over.

'Sorry,' he said. 'I need a bath – badly.'

Everything, he was thinking, everything he touched in the end became ugly. He reversed so violently that the ground seemed to detonate where he rammed the wheels, and tiny stones were thrown back from the blast like a crowd of onlookers scattering in all directions.

A TASTE OF HEAVEN

It was a long drive and, all the way down to Devon, Jess sat in the front of the car next to Daddy. They listened to 'Take a Chance on Me', because Mummy wasn't there, and then *Peter and the Wolf*, because Granny'd given it to her.

'Remember to be quiet around Grandpa,' Daddy said.

Grandpa once chased her with a garden hose. But he was ill last Christmas. He went to hospital. It made his face go funny, like a mistake that couldn't be rubbed out.

'Is he better?' she asked.

'He's getting better. You'll just have to help Granny and be a good nurse.'

When they arrived, Millie jumped up and licked her ears and her nose. Millie, Millie, Millie.

Don't get her overexcited, Daddy said.

Millie's fur had brown patches like spilled chocolate. She ran round in circles and jumped in the air. 'Manor House' it said on her collar. Jess was teaching her to do tricks.

'Millie,' Granny said. 'That's enough!'

'Can she be mine?' Jess asked every time, and Granny

would say, 'Of course, while you're here, she's yours. Look – she loves you.'

Granny's house was big, through gates and up a drive; it looked tidy as a doll's house with three rows of windows and pillars round the front door, a place to scrape your shoes. Inside, it was cool as trees and smelled of honey. In the hall there was a big dimply gong and a stick with a leather ball to bash for dinner. In the dining room there was a wooden box Granny's uncle brought her back from India. It smelled of Granny inside.

The next morning, when Daddy was getting ready to go back to London, he said, 'Sure you'll be all right?' squeezing Granny's arm.

'Of course we will. Don't worry about us.' Granny was always cheerful.

Daddy put his hand on Jess's head and it felt like a hat. 'Be good,' he said.

For a whole week, she did what Granny did. They collected flowers from the garden to take to church; they visited her friends for cake and squash; they went to the shops. Good as gold, everyone told Granny, and sometimes the old ladies folded a pound into her hand and put their fingers to their lips as if they'd stolen it for her.

There were no children to play with in Granny's village, but she watched children running about on the street where she wasn't allowed to go. Granny called them urchins and devils. Jess was from Clapham Common; different from them as a princess.

For days it was sunshiny. There was cow parsley every-where and hornets buzzing with stings. Grandpa sat in his chair in the garden. Sometimes he walked to the greenhouse with his stick, or to the place where the beans grew to check for slugs. Granny brought out barley water, and bread for the birds. They'd peck the crumbs right up to his slippers.

'One day we'll have a treat,' Granny said. 'We'll go on a picnic.'

'A picnic?'

Sometimes Granny looked at her as if she was stupid, or as if she were telling lies. But the way she said it, *pic-nic*, it sounded made up – a baby word.

'You must have been on picnics?' she said.

'I can't remember.'

'Well, you've had a packed lunch. It's the same thing – but outside, on the grass. We used to go with your daddy and Auntie Margaret all through summer. We'd go to the river and they'd swim. Do you remember, darling?' Granny was talking to Grandpa, whose tongue was at the edge of his mouth. He made a noise like a chair scraping.

Jess loved the idea of Daddy when he was a boy, how good the two of them would have been at playing; not like Auntie Margaret, with her plaits and her glasses.

Daddy used to laugh, saying before he met Mummy he was a country bumpkin. He said Mummy rescued him. But Jess knew he liked Granny as much as she did.

'Can we?' she said about the picnic, because it would be something to tell him.

*   *   *

Granny's kitchen was at the bottom of the house. The cooker stood against the wall, with four hot doors and, on the top, heavy lids that if they fell could chop your head off. The kettle was always boiling. Granny slid the shelves inside like a train driver. They made Grandpa's lunches down there: custard with the skin on it.

Granny had been fussing in the pantry. 'Well,' she said, 'I knew it was there.' She lifted a squeaky basket to the table. It was done up tight with a belt as if there was a cat inside. She flicked at it with a dishcloth. 'We haven't had this out for years.'

Inside there were plates and cups crossed in place, all with the same yellowy pattern of balloons and tiny flowers.

Granny unstrapped a tartan pot, unscrewed the lid and put it to her nose like a flower. 'Urghh – goodness.'

'Can we take Millie?'

'Of course.'

'And Grandpa?'

It wasn't his fault, but she didn't like being on her own with him. Same as she wouldn't go in with turkeys at the farm. She noticed at breakfast time how his thick tongue poked out, slimy as a snail. Granny always said it was rude to eat with your mouth open, but he couldn't help it.

On the day of the picnic, just before they set off, the phone rang. When Granny came back into the room, she was holding her hands like a prayer. She said, 'That was Daddy. And they're fine. Just fine. You've got a baby sister. Isn't that lovely?'

'What's it called?' Jess asked.

'I don't think they've quite decided yet . . .'

She knew they wouldn't use her names, Spike or Spud. She'd wanted a boy. 'They could call it Picnic,' she said to test Granny.

Granny laughed. 'Well, it'll be a birthday picnic, won't it? Shall we go and get Grandpa?'

Granny was wearing her pink shirt and her going-out trousers; she made Grandpa take his cricket hat with the blue ribbon. The skin was rubbing off his nose like glue.

There was a patchwork rug of woollen flowers over the back seat of the car, not long enough to reach under her legs, where the leather was a hot-water bottle. She put her hands behind her thighs to stop them sticking.

'Push her off,' Granny said, when Millie tried to climb on to the hamper next to her. There was a milky drop hanging on the end of Millie's long, thin tongue.

You can only wind the window down an inch, Granny said. Jess pushed her nose into the crack: the smell of heated-up car made her sick.

From where she was sitting she could see the back of Granny's hair, scooped and smooth as ice cream, vanilla-coloured. In the mornings she'd go into Granny's bedroom and watch how, when it was luggy, Granny polished it straight with her silver brush, pushing in the wire pins, tucking it round like a folded sheet. She'd sit on the small butterfly stool and ask Granny to show her again where she kept her pearls: a thin black crocodile box in a drawer of the dressing table. Granny wore them when she got married and when

Grandpa had his photo taken with the Queen. And there was a tin where Granny kept the dressing-up beads, a bracelet with a tiny golden gun.

'Wait. Hang on a minute, darling, I'll come round,' Granny said when the engine stopped, pulling up the handbrake with both her hands. Grandpa was fiddling for his stick.

'Watch your head,' Granny said as she pulled the door and placed a hand on his hat to bend him lower. He'd got his stick in one hand and she grabbed his elbow. He was a turtle, half in, half out.

'I c-n m-n-ge,' his voice growled.

Granny said he forgot his letters, though she could understand him. Jess told her she did French at school. *La table*, *La fenêtre. Je m'appelle*.

'It's exactly the same thing,' Granny said, 'not hard to understand once you know.'

Millie jumped between the front seats and followed him out; Jess held on to the ridges of the hamper so they wouldn't forget her.

'Here we are,' Granny said at last, opening her door, 'out you get.'

Grandpa had begun to shuffle along the track, feeling with his stick for bits of stone. She used to hold him by his finger, but he looked as if he'd topple over if she touched him now. There was fluff like dandelion seed coming from his ears and his nose.

'What a lovely day for it,' Granny said. 'You take the juice, I'll bring the chair and the rug.'

'Is this how you carry a baby, Granny?' she asked, clutching the body of the bottle.

Millie had gone ahead, shaking with excitement. 'She can smell water,' Granny said.

They heard the river in the air like leaves. Along the path there were prickles of yellow flowers that made the air smell of shampoo and washing.

'Watch your feet.'

She'd got her purple flip-flops on that made a pat-pat as she went.

Round a bend in the track, they were able to see all the way up the hill, and then, suddenly, the river too, like a rip in the rock.

'Can we go up there?' Jess said, bursting to run ahead.

'Not that far,' Granny said, 'look, here – this'll do.'

They'd reached a bank and the stream there was slow and brown. Granny was standing in a horseshoe shape of trodden grass and began to set up the chair, testing it with the flats of her hands. Grandpa looked worried but let Granny guide him down.

Millie was away wagging her tail so fast that it hardly registered on the air. Jess wanted to follow her – the water was like treasure – but had to go and help Granny fetch the food.

They came back with the hamper between them, lopsided. Jess was making slits of her eyes so the sun couldn't get in. It was dangerous to look at the sun – but today it took up the whole of the sky. They parked the hamper in the middle of the rug and sat down to unpack it: three parcels wrapped in greaseproof paper, cups for drink, knives and forks with yellow plastic handles. They didn't notice at first the chatter from the river, but there was a single cry which made Granny look up. It could have been an animal or a bird.

But it turned out to be a boy.

His head appeared from under the bank and he was wearing nothing but blue pants. Then a girl arrived, trailing along the path in a black swimming costume, a woman behind her with a floaty scarf tied round her tummy, a carrier bag which she dropped to the ground. Finally a man emerged from where the boy had been paddling, raising himself upright, tall and skinny, wearing big pocket shorts.

Granny held the plates to her chest. 'Drat,' she said under her breath, twisting her head towards Grandpa. 'The garage man,' she said, in a low voice, 'Barry Simmonds.'

The boy had begun chucking pebbles into the water, shrieking to make them hop. Millie was yapping at him. The mother fished in the V-neck of her T-shirt for sunglasses, which she fastened to her face like blinkers. Then she unrolled a towel and lay down on it as if she were going to sleep.

The man stretched to the sky, his legs knobbly with veins. He wore a blue cap on his head, back to front. He touched it when he looked up at them, raising his voice. 'Lovely day!'

Granny lifted her pink arm. 'Yes, lovely.'

Then the man crouched and began to pull things out of the plastic bag.

'Me, me.' The boy was skipping on the spot, holding out his hand.

'Back off, Casey,' the mother said, propped on her elbow. 'Just wait.'

Granny swivelled round on the blanket so that she wasn't facing them and began to unwrap lunch.

The mother had a spiky voice. She patted the ground. 'Lauren,' she said, 'suncream.'

The girl was squatting. She pulled an orange tube from the bag and squeezed paste on to her mother's skin, smoothing it in.

The man rubbed his hands together like a fly.

Granny was busy cutting up the things they'd bought earlier in the week from the butcher.

Mr Woodward wore a white hat and an apron with flecks of blood on it. He'd held out one of the orange balls to Jess, bringing over his other hand to make a box; then he'd blown to put the egg inside.

'Scotched egg,' he said. 'Just like that.'

When Granny divided them into halves and then quarters, the yellow, right in the middle, was green at the edges and crumbled. Jess put a piece all together into her mouth; it tasted like food you'd take to the moon: a whole Sunday lunch.

Granny handed Grandpa a plate with half a pork pie cut into bits for him.

'Your favourite.' The meat was pink and marbly with jelly stuff under the lid. Jess shook her head.

'All the more for us, then,' Granny said.

From where the other people were sitting there was a fizz like an explosion and a fountain of bubbles from a bottle big as a fire extinguisher.

Jess wasn't allowed fizzy drinks except at parties. The juice Granny made was watery pink.

She was thinking about parties and fizzy drinks when the boy came over. He didn't come right up but stood with his hand stuck in a bag of crisps.

'You been in?' he said.

Granny was concentrating on eating, dabbing the corners of her lips every time she took a bite.

'Can you swim?' he asked.

Jess nodded, because she could with one foot on the bottom.

'Going in, then?'

She looked at Granny and then Grandpa, who'd got a piece of kitchen paper tucked into the top of his shirt. Because of the boy, she was embarrassed; Grandpa was acting like a baby.

The boy shrugged and turned away; Millie followed him.

'Millie,' Granny called sharply.

Grandpa started to cough.

'Have you had enough, darling?' Granny said to him. 'Like a nap?'

Jess was edging off her flip-flops; she started to undo the four buttons of her blouse, pulled down her skirt, until she was wearing only her pants and vest, which she tucked in.

'Can I go now?'

'Be careful, darling, won't you. Paddling only. Up to your knees, promise.'

* * *

As soon as she reached the river, the boy was there. But he skipped on past her, along the bank, and began to climb the rocks, up to a ledge, checking all the time that she was still watching him. Then he showed his teeth as if something good was going to happen. He took a deep gulp of air, held his nose, bent his knees, and then sprang out over the river, pulling up his legs. The moment he crashed into the pool below she shut her eyes, rained all over with ice pellets of water.

When she opened them, he was swallowed up. But then he burst out, whooping. 'Bet you can't do that!'

She looked back to where Grandpa had drooped in his chair, the hat slipping from its perch to cross his face.

'Chicken,' he said, and lifted his elbows to beat them on the water.

'I'm going in round the bottom,' she told him.

'Scaredy-cat.'

'Casey!' His mother was up on her elbow again.

He waded out of the pool.

'Don't make so much noise.'

'Is your name Casey?' she asked.

He crossed his eyes and somersaulted backwards into the water.

When he surfaced again she blurted, 'I've got a baby.'

Somewhere bleeping in her head was a dot on the radar telling her that she'd become what in proud voices they'd been calling her for months: a Big Sister. Important.

Casey circled his finger next to his ear to say, *loony*.

She put a toe into the edge of the water and gasped – cold sucked right up her leg. She glanced again over her shoulder. Granny had started to tidy up, folding oblongs of greaseproof paper; then she got to her knees and put a hand to Grandpa's arm, looking under his hat; she turned and raised her hand to shield her eyes.

'You're just a girl,' Casey said dismissively.

In that split second she forgot to be good. She was aware of Granny getting to her feet, but ignored her, and climbed up on to the platform where Casey had been standing. She stood for a second with the furry grass between her toes, and then held her nose quickly like he'd done and, before anyone could stop her, took a flying jump.

She heard Granny shrieking her name, but it was too late. She came crashing through the greenhouse roof, the water slicing to the ends of her fingers and toes. And then she was under, muffled by a blanket, cobwebs of weed suspended and drifting, a glug-glugging of bubbles in her ears and mouth.

She didn't realise she'd touched the bottom until she was pushing back through the ceiling, choking rubbish, trying to keep her chin on the surface of the water like an egg on a spoon, scrabbling with her hands and feet towards the bank, then coming smack against two trunks in the water. Her hair was plastered across her eyes, but she could see by the shiny costume, the twin thighs glistening with diamonds, that it was the mother. She stood with a hand on her hip, and leaned over to yank Jess by her elbow, telling her off.

'Out you get from there. You've given your gran a right shock.'

The daughter, watching from the towel, had perked up. Her mother's hand was iron.

When Jess looked up towards the bank, what she saw was a painting from an old book: Jesus, *outside the tomb*. The man was on his knees, hugging Granny from behind round her pink shirt, where she was slumped forward. Grandpa was in his chair beside them, his arms and his stick waving like a daddy-long-legs.

'It's OK, she's all right,' the man said when Jess made a bubbling noise running to get there.

Granny's head jerked forward like a cat being sick.

'Don't try and talk. Not for a minute,' he was saying. 'Deep breaths. Take your time.'

When Granny lifted her face, her eyes were glassy, her lips slack.

Jess was shivering, her vest stuck fast to her skin, her knickers dragging with river.

'Don't ever—' Granny started saying, but then Grandpa made a whimper and Granny turned towards him, reaching out to take his arm.

'There now,' the man said, getting to his feet awkwardly, 'everyone's all right.'

Casey was triumphant, flicking his fingers as if he knew she was going to cry any minute. *Nobody loves you, everybody hates you* . . . She couldn't hold it in any longer. Her face broke.

'Come here,' Granny said, melting suddenly, still holding Grandpa's hand, but reaching to take her in. 'I didn't mean to be cross. But you gave us a fright. A terrible fright,' and she hugged her to her bones, making a purple print all down her shirt front.

'Thank you so much, Barry,' she was saying over Jess's shoulder, her voice trembling right through her. 'I can't thank you enough. How silly of me. How terribly lucky you were there. Oompfh.' She made the sound of a cushion being squashed, and held Jess at arm's length. She was trying to laugh, wiping her nose, but she was still shaking and Barry had to help take things back to the car.

The taste of the picnic stayed in the back of her throat for a long time: mostly the Scotch egg, but also the river, and then the sky – its startling blue – and the cracks the sun made in it.

They agreed they wouldn't tell, only that they'd had a picnic just like Daddy used to. But the story was bound to come out later, linked as it was to her sister's birthday: how she'd been showing off to a boy; how Granny, who'd watched her drop from view as if she was on a see-saw, had choked on a piece of pie and been rescued by the man from the garage, who happened to be there and happened to have seen a programme on the Heimlich manoeuvre.

It was a lovely day, nonetheless, Granny insists. One of those days like heaven.

As soon as she says the word, her eyes fill, because it reminds her of Grandpa. 'I wonder if you remember him,' she says, 'before he got ill? He was such a clever man. He was so handsome. And so glad he came with us that day. His last picnic. He wouldn't have wanted to stay at home for the world. Not miss out on the fun.'

GENTLEMAN SEEKS

Not long after he'd started working for the duke, Eustace Webber had given up on holidays. The odd opportunity to go abroad came with the job: once, he'd driven His Grace and wife to the South of France, ferrying them from *cave* to *cave*, from one dilapidated château to the next.

Thirty years' faithful service he'd given since then; and yet in this, the year of his retirement, it was obvious even to him – despite the bedsit he'd been given in the East Wing – that his continued presence was beginning to grate. His Grace would hang his head wearily every time he passed him in the corridor, and, after various efforts at replacing him had foundered – one turned out to be a drinker, another a scoundrel – a recruitment agency had now been brought in to speed things along. The first thing they'd mentioned was the importance of helping previous incumbents move on.

So Buckleigh, in this case, had been a last resort, some-where to go to preserve his dignity. 'A little holiday,' he announced, and left it at that.

Propped up against the bar of the Red Lion at two in the afternoon, he had the barmaid, Shelley, at his mercy.

'Almost thirty years ago, that was,' he was saying, as she stood drying glasses. How amazed he'd been then to find the village intact, a picture postcard of itself; those wood pigeons in the morning blowing their pipes; the way the air moved in exactly the way he'd remembered it. Like a field of handkerchiefs.

The idea to go back to Buckleigh had first occurred to him in 1977. He'd just been demobbed and was delighted to have secured his first civilian situation: Hallwood House in Northamptonshire. He'd also met a girl, Sheila, a god-daughter of his mother's, an ex-dancer. He was forty and she was twenty-six, though by the time he met her, she'd already been divorced. Being the romantic sort, he thought she'd be susceptible to the spirit of nostalgia. It was the first time he'd been back there since the war. *Would she come and help him celebrate? Little drive out of town?* He collected her from Norwood in the hired Bentley and drove the five hours non-stop, door to door.

'And this is where we stayed,' he said to Shelley, 'hasn't changed a bit. It did the trick: got the ring on her finger (much good it did me): that's another story. Anyway, what I'm really talking about, you understand, is thirty years before *that*. Before you were born 1944 or so. I daresay before your parents were born.'

Shelley smiled weakly; Eustace was beginning to slur his words.

'An evacuee, I was, from London. I'd never seen anything like it.'

What he found extraordinary, he said (though Shelley was making little effort to disguise her boredom) was the fact that in the intervening years, it had gone on just the same without him.

'How incidental are our lives,' he declared.

If Eustace had stinted himself on holidays in the past, he was making up for lost time. This was his sixth visit in less than a year. He'd stayed in the pub at first, but soon discovered the noise kept him awake at night; and despite the ban, he could smell smoke in the wallpaper and the pillows on the bed. Someone had recommended he try Mrs Eastcott, who'd started doing B & B in the square. He'd found her house so accommodating, the novelty (in his current predicament) of having somewhere welcoming such a relief, that he didn't hesitate to book himself in with her again, and again.

Something about the density of her brown wool skirt as it hugged her knees, the swish the lining made when she busied herself around him, put him at ease. He liked the cosy pinkness of her cheeks and, when she sat down, he watched her little feet, misshapen from bunions like a camel's.

Mrs Eastcott would hand him a glass of sherry in the evening, at first hesitating to join him by the fire, but finally relenting, slipping over to sit in the other chair.

'Funny, as you get older,' he'd say, 'how you remember things from when you were small, clear as day.' The knot that tied the label to his coat lapel, he was thinking, the baskets of yellow and purple flowers that awaited them on the station platform. He sucked from the glass and coated his teeth with the sweet liquid before swallowing.

'Until I came down here,' he said, 'I'd never seen a cow. Or a horse.'

'I can't imagine that,' she said.

'I drew my mother a cow. Its udders. I took particular care. They came down way below its feet.'

In the end the letter had never reached her. He was too embarrassed to say he hadn't been able to remember the address. But he'd hung onto the drawing, kept it in the Festival of Britain box with his Morse code book, his passport and his pocket watch.

Every now and again his mother still entered his dreams like the young Queen, the coconut of the oil she used in her hair. Sometimes she'd be stretching out her hand from the kitchen door to call him in from the back garden. Sometimes she was smoothing her stockings, ready to go out.

When Eustace woke that last morning, the sheets were damp and rucked uncomfortably around his neck. He was short of breath, his mouth dry as if it had been stuffed with sacking in the night.

Downstairs, the kitchen smelt of vinegar. Mrs Eastcott was making him poached eggs. Soldiers to dip. His stomach was tight, hard as a pebble.

She resumed proceedings cheerily as if the conversation from the night before had never stopped.

'They've a sale today,' she said, stirring sugar into his tea for him. 'Village hall. Local farmer. Tragic, it was. Old family,

Bradstocks.' She puckered her face and pushed her head forward, lowering her voice confidentially. 'He was burned to death – early this year. It was his wife –' Mrs Eastcott tapped a spoon on the rim of her cup.

'I knew her. Alma. She worked in the bank. Wouldn't harm a fly. But he – Dennis, her husband, Dennis – she caught him. Carrying on, with a woman worked in the Lion.' Mrs Eastcott looked across at Eustace and then away, fumbling with the lid of the hot-water jug.

'A crime of passion, isn't that what they call it? Put her away, though,' she said a little defensively. He registered the flush rising in her soft cheeks.

Since the fiasco of his marriage, his dealings with women, much like his days off, had been scant.

The duke kept Viagra on his bedside table. He would recommend it to Eustace. As if that had been a problem. No shame in it, the duke would say, men in their prime, they're all taking it in town – little boost for the battery. Eustace had no time for drugs, although he was always discreet about the times he picked His Grace up from town, girls in tow, high as kites in the back of the Chrysler; or the time he found him alone, naked, gibbering underneath the stairs with a box of Quality Street.

His few half-hearted attempts at courtship had been abetted by a stable manager, with whom he'd been friendly for a while. It had been more of a joke and a dare between them one night, playing cards – the suggestion: *Gentleman seeks.*

* * *

From the phone conversation and her boarding school voice, Eustace had imagined Mavis Smithers in a tailored suit, sharp shoes that could do damage if hurled – the tiny imprint of a heel like a pebble aimed at a forehead.

She'd told him that after secretarial college she used to model hands: knitting patterns, hand cream, nail polish.

'I'm mad about vintage cars,' she said when they met. He'd come to collect her in the green Jaguar, which he kept in running order for the duke. She was shorter and wider than he'd hoped, with an orange chiffon scarf at her neck. Her hair was vermilion, her scalp showing through in sugar-mouse pink.

He'd specified 45–50 and when she turned up, looking a decade older – older than he was – it was hard to be gallant. She hadn't aged well: her skin was coarse with powder. She got into the seat heavily and when she turned to smile her breath was sickly sweet. Almond. Alcohol.

He'd drawn up in front of Debenhams, deciding that he had no choice but to go through the motions. 'I know a tea shop. Nice little place.'

They'd sat in the window with a plastic poppy in a thin funnelled vase. He spilt his tea on the paper tablecloth and noticed the tea-coloured blotches on the backs of her slender hands. She'd taken off her coat and arranged it around her chair, its white fur collar lying like a cat along the back.

'You don't see fur so often nowadays,' he said.

'Not Animal Rights, are you?'

'Not at all. My mother had one with big furry buttons.' He laughed nervously and began to heap sugar into his tea.

'I've not done this kind of thing before,' he said.

'No?' She shrugged. 'Neither have I, really.'

Then she darted him a look. 'You're not married, are you?'

'No.' He shook his head. 'I was,' he added, 'it didn't work out.'

'I'm sorry.'

'No need.'

When he drove her back to the station, Mavis had refused to budge from the car. He'd said, for form's sake, they'd do this again sometime, that he'd ring. She'd said, *That would be nice, do!* squeezing his arm so that it pinched, leaning in for a kiss. She'd missed his cheek and caught him embarrassingly in the crevice of his neck. He'd pulled away; she squeezed his arm again. Her eyes were filmy and sucked at him. He'd virtually had to push her out of her seat.

Mrs Eastcott was looking at him and he realised he'd got her all wrong. Fooled by the tight slatey curls of her hair, the buttoned-up cardigan, the wobbly line of her chin. Women were all the same: those mollusc eyes waiting for a chance to latch on. He needed to get out of the house.

As soon as he shut the door, he was out in the square. And almost immediately he was caught up in a flow of bodies. The village hall lay twenty yards or so beyond the church. It had been built discreetly lower than the main drag of the village, and the steep slope hid it from sight of the square. Eustace had no particular desire to go to the sale, but with no definite plan in place for his day he found himself easily carried along and, in a moment, face to face with the building.

It was a shock.

There was the pointy wooden roof with a lid you'd be able to lift like a Noah's Ark. There were rails for holding on to. Green paint. He knew that inside the floorboards would be like a ship's deck, the windows, too high to see out of, made of fuzzy glass.

So far, Buckleigh had been a convenience. He'd worn his return to the place like a badge. The two months he'd spent there – at school, building dens, picking cabbages – were, in reality, a blur. But this was something entirely different, quite outside his imagining. His stomach lurched as if he were descending from the thirtieth floor, so disoriented he was unable to recall what clothes he'd put on that morning.

The woman from next door had knitted the cardigan with the mock horn buttons – hippo's teeth – so thick it made it hard to move his arms in his school mac. The belt around his waist was tied in a knot because the buckle had lost its pin.

When he moved towards the hall, he moved as if he were abstracted from the general crowd. Up the stairs, the double doors were pinned back and the concrete threshold stank of dog piss. A large woman blocked his way, brushing wiry hair against his face, the pale flesh of her neck exposed all round like a ruff. Inside, the place was seething. He moved forward, edging his way between slabs of shoulder and jutting baskets, slowly and deliberately as if he were ensconced in an old-fashioned diving suit, the headpiece a golden fish bowl from where he could hear his own breathing and only the faint hubbub of the buffetings in the room.

It was the inside of a wreck. Chests of drawers, wardrobes and unwieldy armchairs were pushed to the back and all along the right-hand side there were trestle tables ranged in parallel lines, laden with boxes of magazines and kitchen implements, the skinny necks of lamps – each table beset by a small mob, nuzzling around like shoals of fish.

There was a rushing noise in his ears he'd experienced only a few times in his life – the noise of drowning, of passing out from the world. He came to a stop, looking up to the platform where the auctioneering gang in their brown overalls were setting up, gesticulating, flicking papers. He was dizzy, his heart ticking from somewhere high above his head.

There was a knot in his pelvis. He'd been holding on the whole journey through, sitting watching himself reflected side on in the black window of the train, his cap pulled down, slumped low in the seat, head bobbing, the fleeting glimpse of a chalk horse stamped on a hill, ribbons of water. Holding on with his legs crossed two times over, all through the ride in the bus that picked them up outside the station – the smell of furry tartan sick.

The women from Buckleigh had arranged them in a line in order of height all along the front of the stage and were checking for lice. He'd let a tiny trickle go, just to see if it would make it any better. But once the knot was loosened, he couldn't help himself: the trickle turned to a flow and then into a gush of yellow stinking liquid that came out of the leg of his shorts like out of a drainpipe, raining loudly on the floorboards so that the woman who was writing on a clipboard turned with her pencil pointing straight at him.

He'd shut his eyes. The whole room had stopped.

'Yes?' a lank, skinny man on a stool asked sharply, lifting his head from his notes. 'Can I help?'

Eustace raised his hands. 'Sorry,' he mumbled, the inside of his thigh cold as a blade.

'Perhaps you'd like a bath?' Mrs Eastcott asked. He'd been back an hour or two and she hadn't managed to get a word out of him. Every now and then she surfaced from the kitchen to feed the fire, and then, around six, she brought out the bottle of Harvey's, placed it gently on the sideboard.

The sound appeared to rouse him. He shook his head and made a small animal noise as if from sleep. Then he rose creakily to his feet, wiped his mouth.

'Monday is it, you'll be leaving?' she asked as he made a move to exit the room, a quiver in her voice which she chased with a cough.

He turned back towards her from the other side of the door. 'I'll be out of your hair.'

'No trouble, not at all,' she said, colouring.

He smiled wanly at the pressure in her voice, meeting the two trembling weights of her eyes. Then he gave her a salute, clicked the heels of his shoes and turned, counting in relief the steps as he climbed away from her.

Eleven. Twelve. Thirteen. Fourteen. *14 Tremadoch Road, SW9.* At the last minute his mother'd tried to drum it in so that he'd have it by heart.

'Be a good boy. I'll see you very soon.' She'd put a cool finger between his neck and his collar and set his cap straight. 'My big brave boy.'

Her red mouth, the bright enamel flowers of her brooch, the black rolls of her hair. All he had to do was post the letter and she'd have come and taken him home, her best flowery dress, the gloves on her hands white as bone.

MRS EASTCOTT

It was odd Mr Webber hadn't come down for breakfast yet. Not like him. But it was a Sunday: natural enough to take advantage of the fact. And perhaps he'd had a busy day yesterday – he'd been out until teatime. She'd leave it a bit.

She couldn't help thinking how nice it felt to have him upstairs. He was cleaner than she'd ever known a man; he smelt of coal-tar soap. It was something she noticed: how people brought their own smell into the house. She took care to replace the air freshener in the lounge and in the upstairs bathroom: it was the price paid for having strangers in. Worst were the couples in the double room, the smell of wrestling, of unfinished business. And it was distasteful the way they'd leave a bed, unmade, shaken up. Sometimes she put on rubber gloves to change the sheets and averted her eyes in case she saw a mess. She liked those couples best who expressly chose the twin.

She'd got used to putting Mr Webber in her favourite room, the small double overlooking the square. She'd chosen a honeysuckle wallpaper and painted the window seat in white gloss, plumped a lacy cushion to one corner. The room reminded her of her mother – it contained the residue of furniture her mother had left her: the mahogany chest of drawers, the pinstriped nursing chair, a pink and green vanity set and the eiderdown with its May-queen flowers.

Sometimes, when she was empty of guests, Mrs Eastcott would open the window and perch on the edge of the bed. It was peaceful in there. The room was high up and it didn't take much of a breeze for the air to rush in, sluicing down the angular walls and ceiling, nudging at the inverted light shade. *Do the dusting for me*, she'd think. On days when she woke up too early, she'd wrap herself in her dressing gown and go in there to look down on the square, listening for the clink of the milk float, making herself tearful: the way it hummed, always positive, just like Brian, her husband, used to be. Or on dark evenings in winter, when the ground would be shiny with rain, she'd spy on the boys who gathered under the lamp by the old pump.

In the kitchen the clock pulsed: half past nine. This morning she was making an effort to avoid looking up at it. Like the time she'd spent with Brian, on the ward, waiting for the nervous bleep of the machine.

Ten years was a long time to be on your own.

With other guests, the waiting would have been an irritation, a hindrance to getting on. With Mr Webber it was something else: anticipation, perhaps. She looked forward to their morning chats; yet 'looked forward' was too restrained: it had become more than that. Like the first cup of the day, she thirsted for it.

Good Morning. There was a note he'd hit at the base of his voice that stirred the core of her. And then his head would appear around the door, questioning, before he emerged in entirety in his mustard-coloured waistcoat, pulling at his cuffs, twiddling the mother-of-pearl cufflinks, the gleaming conkers of his shoes.

She knew his routine. He had two bristle brushes which he kept upturned on the chest of drawers, and would have shaved already so that his skin would be shining when he came down, a blue hydrangea. He took nothing for granted, standing until she said, 'Have a chair,' and he'd bow slightly and go and sit in the table by the window, where she'd have put a copy of the *Western Morning News*.

If he'd been up with her late at night, the mornings were a strange realignment of formalities. Last night, for instance, he'd told her his first name: Eustace. Not a name that she could bring herself to say, although she tried. It was posh. And yet he always treated her with the utmost respect.

'Very well, thank you, Mrs Eastcott, slept like a log,' he'd say, not at all as if he were beyond her reach.

It was unusual to have a man like that on his own, someone who had no particular purpose – no brewery inspection, no fishing reunion or anniversary. And one who appreciated her little touches: the bowls of pot pourri and scented wood chips in the bathroom. This was his fourth visit in a row and she'd got to know a little bit about him. She was happy, after dinner, to let him sit up with her, in Brian's chair.

*　　*　　*

It was hard to believe that a profession like that still existed, in this day and age, but that's what he was, after the army: head butler eventually, up country, one of those huge stately homes, for the Duke of Somewhere. And he'd been married, once, though his wife had been much younger, flighty, and it hadn't lasted.

He told her how good the family had been to him during that difficult time, how in retrospect he could see he'd gone off the rails. They'd had to stop him driving for six months, got in a special chauffeur. Kept him on though, let him have a suite of rooms in one of the wings; and it paid off for them too: thirty years of loyal service. Eustace was the only one allowed in the morning into the duke's bedroom to give him his pills; saw the state of him some days: excrement – you wouldn't believe it – in the sheets.

Little things Mrs Eastcott noticed about him. Like no dandruff on his collar, the paper-sharp press of his creases. Brian had never been quite the same after the plate was put in, a big dent in his forehead like an old enamel jug. She was always having to straighten him up, wiping egg from his beard before they left the house.

Perhaps it was the difference that took her unawares. Mr Webber was like a man in a book, the man, when she was a little girl, who would have been going off to work with a hat and an umbrella to an office in a city. Brian was her own kind. They'd been at school together, married young. He was near retirement when he had the accident in the warehouse; they'd let him stay on, part-time; and he was good around the house. He played cricket in the summer for the pub and, like her father, had been a stalwart of the band. Euphonium. He had the perfect build for it: short legs, a barrel of a chest.

There were certain things she missed about being married: the way people didn't fuss after you; those quiet intimacies of morning tea, a nip of something before bed. And the balance of a room when someone else is there; the worst thing: the lack of balance when they're gone.

She found herself, even after all this time, saying his name under her breath like a prayer. But there'd been no passion, no slow undressing. Not like books or at the pictures – they'd been more brother and sister.

There were stories about Mr Webber's time in Buckleigh that she would encourage out of him. She kept his glass filled tactfully. He told her about the girls who came to poison the rats. How the rats were congregating in barns and hayricks and had begun to swarm, a river of them, flowing in a black column straight across the fields towards town.

And men were called out with metal pipes and spades, whatever they could lay their hands on, so that when the rats began to arrive in Buckleigh they were ready for them.

'Dripping with sweat – bash, bash, bash – fast as their heads popped up. And a gang of us boys, stuffing them into sacks as quick as they could whack 'em, twenty at a time – some half alive, others stiff as toast.'

'I hate a rat's tail,' Mrs Eastcott shuddered. 'I absolutely hate it.'

'Those Land Girls hardly blinked an eye. Held them up by their tails. Handfuls of them. Like they were collecting radishes.'

'Like a top-up?' Mrs Eastcott asked, and tipped the bottle so that the liquid fell like a coil into the glass. 'They'd love to hear your stories in the village. They'd have you in at the school in a flash.'

That last time, the shock of recognition as she watched his features fall like a mirror into place. She wanted everything to be right for him, no guests who'd come back late and disturb him, no young couples making animal noises all night.

She'd found herself looking forward to 9th September, drawing a flower head around the date in her calendar, and writing *Mr Webber* neatly with an arrow over the next page and writing it again on the Monday, though this time with a question mark: *Mr Webber goes?*

She was thinking, Brian would never have allowed himself to sleep in; she'd never have been able to treat him. She was smiling to herself at the idea in her head – how decadent he'd have thought it! – reaching for the pony tray, its little wicker fence to keep the things in place. She went to the glass cupboard and took down the heather-sprig teapot, which she used for best, took a cup and saucer from the sideboard, the matching jug and sugar bowl, gave them all a shine with the drying-up cloth. Laying the linen napkin with its four-leaved clovers, its flying orange geese, was something her mother would have done. And she'd bought a box of sugar cubes for the miniature silver tongs they'd had as a wedding present. The kettle had boiled. She swilled the pot. While she waited for the tea to brew she sat down with a hand laid over her belly to settle her stomach. Her handbag was on the fridge and she reached over for it, took out a deep pink lipstick and without looking in a mirror smoothed its tip along the upper outline of her mouth, then pressed her lips together like a butterfly, rolling the colour in. She fluffed her hair around her ears, lifted the apron over her head like leather tack.

Casting a final eye over the tray, she adjusted the cloth and then she grasped it to her, arms full width, feeling the muscles and the bones as if she were working a contraption, and backed through the narrow door into the pit of the steep stairway.

As she climbed the stairs, blind beneath the tray, she imagined him turning in surprise – pleasant surprise – his striped pyjamas open at the neck, her sitting gently on the edge of his bed.

She had crept up earlier, pretending to herself that she was checking the adjacent room – the mantrap of a floorboard that groaned as she passed – and had listened for a moment at his door. Not a flicker. This time she made no effort to disguise her ascent and stood determinedly in the same spot, heard herself say cheerfully, 'Morning!'

There was no response. She cleared her throat and adjusted the tray on to the bracket of her knee, knocked hastily to keep her balance.

'Morning, Mr Webber!'

Still no answer. She felt foolish, cross with him for making her look a fool. It was too late to retreat. She pressed on, taking the bulbous handle of the door and turning it, grabbed the tray almost simultaneously and nudged into the room.

'Morn—'

The word reared in her mouth and the tray rocked forward, sliding crockery to its wicker edge. And then, as if in slow motion, the milk came toppling over, flung to the swirly carpet, snow melting into the pile. The cup broke clean in two, its saucer rolling under the bed, and then the teapot lid – hats off – tea leaves spattering like ants in a jungle.

Her arms dropped like chains; the tray hit the floor. She turned away into the corridor, aghast, frantically taking in the paper border of Egyptian hieroglyphs, the gilt frames of a pair of Constables, the light switch. But every detail she strove to fix swooned at her now as if they were on a sinking ship.

'Mr Webber?' she said in the corridor like a child locked in a dark cupboard.

She gulped, clenched her teeth and forced herself to go back in. Slowly she put her hand up to her mouth, bit a finger.

The eiderdown was turned over. The man she saw, who'd been so spruce, so well-turned out, now lay – it made her think of a pig, a pantomime – flat out on the bed. He was wearing a red cotton dress, its zip gaping open at the side with pink flesh showing through like raw chicken. The short sleeves were stretched at the seams with little hyphens of stitches over the tops of his arms, pale and freckled. One arm, a cantilever, out from the bed. His legs were dead straight and hairless, goosefleshed. There were maroon socks on his feet, and elastic braces for holding them up. Drunk? Asleep? But she knew not, by the yellow-grey pallor of his skin.

'Brian,' she whispered, when she meant to say 'God.' The name Eustace also sprang to mind, and the thought, suddenly, that maybe, after all, it might be a woman's name.

Then she heard a tinkling sound, the sink in the corner, gurgling, lifting a weight of scum and suds, about to brim over. She hurried across the room and, with half an eye out for the body as if it might yet spring up from the bed, turned off the idling tap. She could see the water wasn't draining properly, something was blocking it, not the iron filings of a chin, but finer, longer hair, like weed in a pond.

There was a sweaty puddle of dark carpet around the pedestal. The drip continued like a clock. She stood facing the bed. His skin was waxy, overblown, magnolia. She swallowed. The burden of what she would have to do felt as if it would bring the ceiling crashing down on her. Doctor. Police. She moved in tiny steps towards the bedside. A red dress with flowers of blue and green. It was something her mother might have worn, something from the war.

'Mr Webber?' she said, still hoping that it was a terrible, unfortunate joke and that he would come round. She put a hand out to the fabric where it touched his knee, swallowing again. Perhaps she should take the dress off? She drew the hem a little upward, looking at his face, his blear marble eyes, rolled to the roof of their sockets, and could see where his tongue had pressed forward, bluish with a bubble of spit where it met the serrated edge of his teeth. The dress would lift as far as the waist and no further: no way of getting it off but by embracing him, lifting him upright in a semi-dance. She shivered.

But she was curious. Who would see her now if she looked?

There was a boy at school, Tom Brookes, who got taken away in the end because he wouldn't stop showing the girls. It was like a little slug or a snail, that was all she remembered, and the way they used to run to the teacher, 'Miss, Miss – he done it again!' covering their mouths like their mothers did, as if they were going to be sick.

And Brian, he did it without a word to her, not roughly or anything, but as if, *we'll do it and then we'll draw a veil*, as though it never happened. She let him turn from her and tuck himself away. Once or twice she spotted him in the bath, but he'd always rise up, like Neptune, the cloudy water around him and a tidal wave against the taps, covering himself with his hands.

She lifted the hem as if there was something still living in there, a snake that might jump out. She peeped. Mr Webber's legs were dead straight and between them, in a warm, soft nest of tawny hair, there was a little bald mouse, its eyes tight shut, dreaming of how things might have been, a soldier, a lion.

FEATHERS

Stan had joined the dramatic society a year or two after Beryl had died, to be busy, and, yes, perhaps in time, to meet someone. It was a surprise, even to Stan, when he proved to have a talent for it, especially, as it turned out, for comedy. His dancing stole the show in a production of *Abigail's Party*.

The night that Sheila Delaney turned up, there were just three weeks to go before the opening night of the summer production, *The Wizard of Buckleigh*. Bertram, the director, was delivering one of his regular lectures on attitude and attendance – the assembled cast, mostly teenagers, ranged against the far wall and flagrantly occupied in other conversations.

Sheila at this point was a figure grappling with the swing doors. She fell into the cavernous hall with a little shriek of surprise.

'Might as well be directing synchronised swimming,' Bertram was saying. He flung his script to the floor, turning on his heel and reeling almost – to gulps of laughter – into Sheila's arms.

It was remarkable to Stan how quickly Bertram was able to recover his composure. 'Welcome,' he said, inspecting the newcomer.

The group had fallen silent. No one recognised who she was or where she'd come from.

'Sheila Delaney,' the woman announced, taking in the assembled company with the beam of her smile. 'I've wanted to be a chocolate button from the age of five.'

Apart from Stan, the only other adult left in the cast was Moira. She'd eventually conceded the part of Dorothy to the all-singing Bradley girl, and bagged for herself the 'meatier' role, as Bertram put it, of Wicked Witch. Moira wished now she'd had her hair done that week: there was a white Plimsoll line along her roots. It was obvious to her that Sheila's was professionally highlighted. The coat she was wearing looked posh too – camel or camel mix – down to her ankles, with a large shawl collar, and her shoes were black patent with a square fabric bow across the bridge. Moira wondered how old she was – fifties? – pleased at least to see, each time Sheila swept the room with her smile, how neglected her teeth were.

Teeth aside, there was no doubt that Sheila was attractive enough for Bertram to have a go; he needed cheering up, he wouldn't be able to help himself.

Although Sheila had insisted that she hadn't come for a speaking part – she wanted a chance to find her feet in costumes and make-up – she would enjoy coming to rehearsals.

And it was at the very next meeting that Stan overheard Bertram asking, 'Fancy a drink?'

Sheila was rummaging in the big laundry basket. She jumped, her hands spread like a butterfly. 'Me?'

Stan contrived to follow them out as far as the car park, watching Bertram manoeuvre her along over the bridge to the quieter pub at the bottom end of town, The Lamb, his arm formally extended around her lower back.

After Beryl died, Stan refused to go to chapel. In the last six months of her illness, he'd done enough praying to last a lifetime. Beryl hadn't liked him drinking and now – it was common knowledge – he was drinking to make up for lost time. *Better than a friend, swifter than a prayer.*

A year after her death, nothing had got any easier for him. He couldn't get over the idea that she was watching. She was everywhere in the house: the cushions were hers, the pictures, the curtains; it was her thimble collection, her engraved glasses in the cabinet. Even the bottle of washing-up liquid on the window ledge, or the soap powder he used, reminded him of her – pairs of rubber gloves under the sink, as if she'd taken off her hands and left them behind.

Barry, their son, had discovered him one day out in the dark in the yard, drinking and weeping, and offered – since his own wife had left him by then – to move back into the house. It suited them both. Although they worked together all day – in 1990 the garage was reregistered as Simmonds & Son – they were careful to keep their social lives distinct. Stan had the band and the dramatic society; Barry, like his mother, was more involved in the parish council – to the point, last year, of becoming Mayor – and he'd kept up with chapel too, lending his baritone to the choir.

But the dynamic had changed recently. Barry'd started

seeing someone new – turning up some mornings for work barely shaved – and Stan, conversely, was beginning to acknowledge that the chances of him meeting anyone at his age, despite his best efforts, were remote.

So he was caught off guard when, during a break in the following week's rehearsal, he overheard Bertram congratulating himself to Moira on the caution he'd shown. He was comparing Sheila's smile to a lamping beam and did an imitation of himself as a badger, escaping into the hedgerow, grey and lumbering.

'If she ever suggests a drink again, you're coming with me: reinforcements,' he said to Moira, who'd gone auburn in town and was back to her ebullient self.

Another week on, Stan was putting a wet comb through his hair and brushing his teeth. He was looking forward to the run of dress and technical rehearsals. It wasn't so much the anticipation of public recognition – the gratifying congratulations when people came to pay him for their petrol – it was the chance, he realised, to be around Sheila, a woman who was beginning to exert a certain fascination.

'Open up a bit,' she was saying to Stan backstage, her own mouth gaping in sympathy and getting so close to him that he could smell the mix of cabbage and chocolate on her breath.

'Goodness,' she said. 'You've hardly got any lips.'

Stan was sweating in an all-over lion suit, his eyes darting like two chickens in a coop. He made a supreme effort to unlock his jaw as Sheila applied herself to twisting up the dog-end of the coral lipstick. He hated exposing his missing front tooth. She was taller than him, her body encompassing him in a field of electricity. He concentrated on keeping absolutely still, hardly breathing, pressing the balls of his feet into the cool lino of the floor. All he could hear was the whooshing sound of sawing from the hall, the teeth of the saw, the prickly smell of emerald-green paint – the scenery, as usual, scrabbled together at the last minute.

It was almost ten years ago to the day since Beryl had died and this was as close as he'd got to any other woman.

Not strictly true.

There'd been a few aberrations, after Robert from the band had told him about the place in Plymouth – discreet, well-run – and pressed a number on him. Plymouth seemed, in many ways, less of a betrayal of Beryl. Out of sight and mind.

He wondered now if Sheila could tell. He was biting the inside of his mouth where there was already a painful ulcer. He realised what it was, reminding him of Harbour Road: it was the smell, an exact replica, the sweet dampness of talcum powder. If he closed his eyes, he could see the three-quarter bed, the lilac sheets, the tasselled lamp draped with a blood-red scarf. He could even taste whisky in his mouth: the half-bottle of White Horse he'd down to get him in there, his mouth dry as carpet.

The second or third time, he'd found a regular place to park and he knew the routine, undressing without a word, putting his clothes on the plastic office-type chair. He'd hold his shirt by the shoulders and the cuffs and shake out the creases in the way he'd seen no other person but Beryl do; carry his trousers over his forearm like a waiter, place his shoes under the legs of the chair so that the toes just touched each other. Then he'd sit on the edge of the bed and the girl would kneel by him, direct and pragmatic.

Chickens, he was thinking, desperate to divert himself as Sheila smeared rouge into his cheeks: the way they moved like busy housewives bundled up on market days, shapes indeterminate under headscarves and coats and bags all tucked about them. Chickens pecking and skittering about the yard with nothing on their minds but the drill head of seed and filling their gullets pellet by pellet. It helped in particular to bear in mind the shit that smeared the back of their white, soft feathers. Foul. The pun was a nice distraction: fowl, he repeated to himself, spelling the word in pink cursive neon. Except that, in congratulating himself, he'd lowered his guard and the whiteness, the softness of the feathers began to brush against his face – Sheila's airy blouse, tickling his nose with the scent again of heady flowers. He'd have liked a drink.

It was when they were getting changed that Stan brought out the eggs for her. His four chickens were producing three eggs between them, he said, and he could afford to be generous. He was sorry he'd run out of egg boxes and handed over a Tupperware container, each egg inside carefully wrapped for her in a green napkin from the pub.

'What a lovely thing to do,' she said, in front of everyone. 'How sweet of you!'

Stan intercepted a look from Bertram to Moira.

'You're very welcome,' he said. 'Glad they're appreciated.'

She was reaching inside her handbag and held out her purse.

'Let me give you something?'

Stan shook his head. 'I've more than I know what to do with.'

'Well, a drink then. Let me buy you a drink?'

It was silly, but Stan was shaking when he carried the drinks over to the small round table and set them down, her white wine spilled around the base of her glass, his port and lemonade.

He'd brought her up to the Red Lion and they were sitting privately in the little alcove.

'I'd love to be able to keep chickens,' Sheila said enthusiastically, 'being in the country, seems silly not to. But they say you get rats.'

Stan was reasonably confident on the subject of poultry. 'Not a problem, really, not if you keep the food locked away, keep them a bit hungry. They don't need a deal of space. I've only a yard out the back, a patch of grass, a little coop. They do all right.'

He began to shoulder himself out of his jacket, arranging it around the back of the chair.

'They recognise you in the end. They'll cluck around your feet, let you stroke them.'

'Do they have names?'

Stan shifted in his seat. 'You give them names to tell one from the other.'

'I think that's sweet,' she said, 'tell me?'

'Oh,' Stan said, cataloguing on his fingers, not quick enough to lie. 'There's Bertie, Boop, Dot and – er – Sheila.'

'Sheila? That's my name!'

'Names,' he said hastily, 'pulled out of a hat.'

Although it was August, it was damp in the lounge and Nigel, the barman, had come over to ask if they'd like the electric fire. Sheila did feel the cold, she said, and he'd gone off to fetch it from the shed. It buzzed when he set it up in the hearth, as if it had been kicked awake, releasing a smell of burning hair, and then settled down, hummed orange, its coil compelling in the drab light of the room.

'Is there a Mrs Simmonds, then?' Sheila asked coyly.

'Oh.' Stan glanced up. 'Beryl. Yes. She got cancer. Ten years ago. It was very quick in the end, sudden.'

'I am sorry. That must've been terrible for you.'

Stan's hands were two brackets; he let them fall away from each other.

'I live with my son, Barry. He works with me at the garage. You might have got petrol from us – Bradcott Road?'

'I tend to go the Exeter way, if I have to. Do you live in Buckleigh?'

He nodded. 'South Street, off the square.'

'I've a soft spot for the place – came here years ago,' Sheila said. 'But Ralph, he wanted land.'

'Doesn't suit everyone, I'm sure. Barry, my son, married a girl, took off soon as blink at you. Town wasn't big enough.'

'Funny, that,' Sheila interrupted. 'It *is* such a tiny place – and yet they call it *town*.'

'Market charter, that's what makes it a town, I think, strictly,' Stan said, relishing for a moment the opportunity to impart knowledge. 'Big enough for the likes of me, anyway. Nice place to retire.'

'You can't be that old?' Sheila said.

'Not long to go now. Next year.' He glanced at her, to acknowledge what he took to be a compliment. 'Don't feel it, though. Young as the one you feel, that's what they say, isn't it?'

Sheila laughed and Stan raised his glass, took a sip. Momentarily his tongue stuck where for years he'd lived with a lost tooth.

'For you, then, is it – the actor's life?' he asked.

Sheila swilled wine against the sides of her glass. 'It brings back memories,' she said, 'that's for sure.' And then, looking straight at him, lowering her head, she whispered, 'I was a dancer, once, you see. Dancer-trained.'

'Really?' he said, lightly as he could. 'A dancer?'

'Folies-Bergères,' she said, pronouncing the French self-consciously. She was watching his face. 'It was all done with feathers – very artistic.'

'I'm sure,' he said, playing with the collar of his shirt and attempting to disperse an assembly line of women dangling their legs.

'Before I got married, of course. My first husband knocked such dreams on the head.'

'Married?'

'Four times.'

'Have you any hobbies?' he asked, a slight cracking to his

voice. She was obviously racy. He was wondering if those sorts of dancers wore knickers.

Sheila flashed her eyes. 'I'm a sucker for antiques,' she said.

Stan was holding on to the edge of the table and said, with relief and surprise, 'Me too. *Antiques Roadshow.* Never miss it.'

He and Beryl used to sit down together ritually on a Sunday evening to watch the programme. He'd built her intricate shelves to display her hundred or so porcelain thimbles.

'We liked an antique,' Stan said, to fill what had turned into an awkward silence.

'Well,' Sheila said emphatically, 'I may be a bit of an old antique, but I'm a girl at heart.' She forced a little laugh and shoved a beer mat towards the centre of the table.

It sounded like a line from a play. For a moment Stan was alarmed: he couldn't place the reference; then he worried he'd said something tactless.

'I'm teasing,' she said, 'you're a gentleman, I can see that.'

Stan blenched a little as she went on, 'My mother would adore you. She loves a gentleman. She keeps scrapbooks: she's got all my photographs – old boyfriends from school, right through. She loves to have a picture. Says you can tell so much from that.'

Sheila was animated now, her face reflecting the glow of the wine glass under her chin like a buttercup. 'Miss Babs and Miss Sylvie used to say the Academy was the perfect training for a wife. One of the best shows we did, in Black-pool, for the telly: Mike Yarwood – remember him? He always said he could've taken his pick blindfold – any one of us – and know he'd not be disappointed. I'd a photo of him, too, signed – Mother'll have it somewhere.'

'Where's she to?'

'Oh, Mother stayed in London. You'd never get her out.'

'I'd like to have seen you dance,' Stan hazarded, enter-taining again images of dancers and feathers. He smoothed condensation from the belly of his glass.

'Really? How sweet.' Sheila straightened her shoulders and blinked deeply. 'How really sweet.' And then she added impulsively, 'Why not come and see me? Have a look at the furniture. I've sheds full of the stuff. Come and have a coffee? Any time. Come tomorrow – how about that?'

'Oh, I'd like that,' Stan said, 'sometime. Very much.'

Barry was away for nine days, which, this week of all weeks, was bad timing. He'd found one of those last-minute deals, a cheap flight from Exeter all-inclusive; taking the new woman, Debbie, and her kids. It had meant Stan shutting up shop early in the week to get to rehearsals. He was fed up of apologising to people. Think of the rest of the time, he felt like yelling: it was thanks to him that they were open at all.

Although Beryl would have loved grandchildren, he wasn't sure what she'd have made of Barry taking on another man's kids. She'd have worried. But Stan knew himself well enough to detect a touch of envy too. Barry was young enough to have a life ahead of him.

Seize the day. He'd been havering over whether to go or not, and now he banged his mug on the counter. *Why not?* They'd find something to moan about whatever he did. BACK AT ONE he scrawled in capitals on a used envelope and stuck it to the door, pulling down the blind.

Heading west on the road to Bude, the directions she'd given couldn't be faulted. He passed the whitewashed cottage with the yellow door, the converted chapel, and turned in at the signpost, exactly where she'd said, into the rutted lane. A mile down, there was a cob longhouse with a half-barrel of tatty pink geraniums out the front. Peering hesitantly from behind the windscreen, he drew up beside a white pickup and a small blue Renault. Perhaps she'd asked someone else along too?

He was aware of the possibility that he was being watched. He switched off the engine and climbed out of the car, pulling in his stomach, conscious of his posture. As he slammed the door and turned to face the house, he saw her in the shadow of the porchway: she was in her slippers, a man-sized dressing gown, holding back a veil of hair.

'Hope I'm not early?' he said.

'You're fine. Kettle's on.'

She tightened the belt of the dressing gown and motioned him inside, into a narrow kitchen with a dresser along one wall. Opposite, under a dusty window, there was an aluminium sink full of dishes and on the draining board, half a dozen scrubbed-out tins.

'Like a coffee? Tea?'

She was reaching up to a cupboard and brought out a brown jar and two cups. A tufted cat began to roll itself against his legs, tugging at his trousers.

'Tiger,' she said, 'leave him alone! Go through,' she beamed at Stan. 'I'll be with you in a minute.' She indicated the doorway with her elbow and he lowered his head, stepped carefully over the cat. It was dark in the room and for a moment there seemed no way through. He was fenced off by a clumpy table which lay at angles to the rough backside of a chest of drawers. Beyond, there were two sofas ranged parallel to each other, one whose arm spewed coarse horsehair, the other squarer, with a geometric pattern, not dissimilar to the one they had at home.

She raised her voice to him from the kitchen. 'Go and sit by the fire, if you can make your way over – bit of a mess, I'm afraid.' He negotiated the furniture as if he were wading through water, the tops of his thighs pressed by various ledges and arms. The fireplace, when he came to it, was a huge open space. To distract himself from the question of the dressing gown, he craned his head under the lintel into the chimney. Way above, daylight penetrated to reveal treacly patches of tar.

'Bread oven,' she said proudly from the doorway. He extracted his head and watched her make her way over, a mug in each hand, fielding the table, the sofa, with her hips.

'Original. And there's a Bible cupboard up there.' She pointed with one of the mugs to a squat iron door set into the wall, then gestured towards the more battered of the sofas. 'Make yourself room.'

There was a stack of magazines slipping into a depression in the middle of the seat. As he sat, there was a landslide towards him.

'Lovely old place,' he said politely.

'It was Ralph's idea – he was going to do it up, fill the barns and go into business properly.'

There was no ring on the significant finger, though Stan observed a lumpy amber object like a beetle on her right hand.

'I've never been much of a picker, but Ralph wasn't a bad man. He did it for me, moving down here – we used to stay at the Red Lion.'

'Did you divorce – Ralph?'

'Oh no. Nothing like that. Very unfortunate. He's no longer with us.'

'I'm sorry.'

'Oh,' she sighed. 'I'm over it now. Takes time, though, doesn't it. Good to see you. Cheers,' she said.

Stan cleared his throat and raised his mug, extending his lips. Up close, two pinheads of cream floated on the surface, two perimeter rings of fat.

'Do you think I frighten people off?' she asked suddenly.

Stan peered into the room over the mug's heavy circumference.

Sheila was smoothing her dressing gown over her thighs. 'I know it sounds silly, maybe, but I seem to have that effect.'

She paused. 'Bertram: he was so friendly. I feel a bit of a cold shoulder now.'

'I wouldn't take much notice of him,' Stan said, 'he's a bit like that, hot and cold.'

'Do you believe in fate?'

Stan was beginning to feel rattled by her directness. He took a gulp from his mug.

'Everyone – simply everyone told me it was the last thing I should do, burying myself down in this part of the world, and yet all along, something seems to have been pulling me here. I was in my twenties – can you imagine? – and it seemed such a sweet place. Eustace, my second husband – he was evacuated here, during the war (much older than me, of course). He'd not been back until he brought me to stay at the pub, and he was amazed by it – how it had stayed the same. It made a similar impression on me, I suppose, coming from London.'

'D'you miss it – London?'

'Oh I do. The ballet, the theatre, the buzz. Out here, you could go for a year and not see a soul.' She was picking at a torn swatch of fabric on the old sofa. She stopped herself deliberately, as if it were a bad habit of hers. 'So: it's lovely to have some company.'

There was a tremor of excitement in her voice. She'd been balancing on the far arm of the sofa, but now she slipped to her feet.

Stan was attentive, ready to move and follow her if that were required. But she didn't shift from the spot. Instead she began to loosen the knot of her dressing gown.

'You were so kind ...' she was saying, although Stan couldn't make sense of the words – his ears were ringing.

There was a dull landing of material on to carpet like snowfall. From the corner of his eye he saw the edge of a slipper, not the flat unisex slippers she'd been wearing earlier, but – as if by magic – a moulded pair made of grey satin, slightly stained at the toe, a tall gunmetal heel. She twisted round to reach behind the sofa and brought out two sets of feathers, which streamed from her hands and stroked against the sparkly stones and sequins sewn into – what? the gusset? – rising from between her legs. Over her stomach a filmy powder-coloured material stretched to reveal the imprint of a belly button, ripped just beneath the right breast where skin pushed through like dough. A further range of red, green and yellow stones were glued or stitched along the horizontal hourglass that contained her breasts.

'Don't look so worried,' she said softly, 'I won't eat you.'

In his head there was a man in black, arms waving, uttering a hellfire patter of instruction: to act/not to act. Everything was happening too fast. He made no move: his brain in stasis, a fish breathing. He could have stayed there for ever. Like Jesus on the top of the mountain. But after a minute that seemed to stretch impossibly thin, he became aware of movement next to him, her neck and shoulders slouching, a slumping at the waist.

'Nothing's going to happen,' she said wearily. 'Mike's upstairs, having a lie-in. He'll be down in a minute.'

Stan revived and looked at her, appalled.

'My lodger. I always have a lodger. To pay the bills. Mike's used to me.' She stooped down to retrieve the puddle of towelling and he could see the stretch and pull of each breast, the pink lines of her veins like bathroom tiles.

His arm shuddered involuntarily, slopping coffee into his lap.

'Got to make a start,' he said, leaning forward purposefully.

'Don't go now, not like this,' she said, pulling the sides of the dressing gown together.

'I had no idea – That there was – That you – Thank you,' he said, giving up on explanation as she took the cup from his hand.

'Don't leave. I didn't mean to upset you.'

Stan continued to make a move, shrugging and shaking his head.

'I have, haven't I? Let me see.' She was trying to search out his eyes but he'd turned his head towards the kitchen door.

Then she said quietly, 'If you won't stay, will you please just let me have a kiss, a little one, to show we're friends?'

A kiss? His blood ran cold. He hadn't received or given a kiss since Beryl had died. It was the one thing you couldn't pay for, a kiss. *They won't; don't ask*, the woman from Plymouth had said over the phone. And the kisses he'd had from Beryl – a dry brush of the cheek – they were hardly the kisses of his imagination. Those endless nights, after a drink or two, with the TV on, when he'd practise on himself, his arm, his wrist.

The word, when Sheila said it, made him think she knew; it reminded him of compost – rich and dark – the bags he'd buy for tomatoes, the split of tomato skins.

What was she trying to do to him? There was another man upstairs. What could she mean by it? Catchy-kissy: the girls would always scream when you caught up with them.

And yet when he turned in order to decline as politely as he could, not wishing to be rude, what he saw in her face, inexplicably, was a wound – her mouth open, her eyes throbbing. He fell back into the lap of the sofa. She was shuffling forward in her slippers, making birdlike noises. 'You'll let me, won't you?' she asked, plaintively. She reached over to support herself on the arm of the sofa, leaning towards him as he closed his eyes, and then – mouth to mouth – she entered him like the Lady Worm. He had lost all direction, his spine collapsing like a deck of cards.

'Nice.' Into the room a young man's voice rang decisively.

For a second, Stan did nothing. But it was impossible to ignore – a ricochet from a bullet. He unlatched himself with effort from her mouth and swivelled round. Sheila stayed exactly as she was, but one eye squinted towards the corner of the room. Then she put her hand on her hip wearily as if to lever herself up.

'Mike,' she said with no hint of surprise in her voice, and indicating Stan, 'meet Stan.'

'Nice one,' Mike said. He was wearing a tight-fitting leather jacket with shiny zips, and was holding a compact camera. 'Great.'

Stan looked at Sheila and then at Mike in disbelief. A web tightened between the three of them.

'What're you doing?' he demanded.

He got to his feet and patted the top of his head distractedly, rattling for the keys in his jacket pockets. 'What's this all about?'

Sheila looked at him patiently and held out her hand as if she were stopping him from crossing a busy road. 'You look worried. There's nothing to worry about. Nothing at all –'

'I don't want a picture,' Stan said, bewildered.

'I would've asked. Mike's jumped the gun, that's all. I'd have asked and then you wouldn't be worried.'

'What made you think I'd want a picture?'

'I thought, when we talked, Stan, that you'd understand. You're like me: you'd like a souvenir, that's all. A little memento.'

'Of what? Memento!' Stan glared at Mike. Mike hung his head and his dead-straight straw hair fell forward over his face. At the bottom of his drainpipes, there was a pair of outsize trainers with no laces in them.

For the first time in his adult life Stan felt the urge to hit a man, picturing the fist of his hand through a scattering of pulp.

'What's in it for you?' he said.

Mike raised his head and a nose and chin appeared. He was holding the camera behind his back.

'Don't ask me,' he grunted.

'Mike's just helping,' Sheila said. 'Nothing sinister. But if you don't want to participate, that's fine. Just fine.'

'What're you going to do with it?' Stan said, growing more agitated, pointing at Mike's studded belt.

Sheila said, suddenly petulant, 'Don't flap your arms. Why are you flapping? He's not going to do anything. It's for me. It's private.'

'I want you to delete it. Now. So I can see. Come on.'

Mike perked up a bit. 'My camera,' he said. 'You're not touching it.'

'You need permission.'

'Who's gonna make me?' Mike said mockingly, his nose more prominent again.

Sheila was clutching at her dressing gown.

'There's no need for this,' she was muttering, 'for goodness sake. Just a bit of fun.' Then she turned angrily to Stan. 'Don't do your hands like that at me.'

Stan looked at her helplessly and then at his hands. 'What am I doing? You made me kiss you.'

'A kiss, that's all.' She trailed around the battered sofa towards Mike. Stan looked from one to the other: the two of them ranged against him. His eyes were filling with lead. He stumbled backwards, prodded by the furniture like a calf at market, and then – as if he had a calling – he blundered out of the house, the yard, the lane.

They were listening to the sputtering and the whine of the car as Mike took Sheila by the hand.

'I'd give you one,' he was saying. 'Why won't you let me?'

He tugged at her and she followed him up the stairs. 'I'm old enough to be your mother,' she said.

'Doesn't bother me.'

On the landing she eased the camera from his hand. 'Mine,' she said, and then, 'I'm going back to bed. Don't answer the phone.'

'He thought we were at it, anyway – way he scarpered like that. Shame to disappoint him.' Mike was standing four-square in the frame of the door.

'Haven't you got something to do?' she said. 'Haven't you got a job to be getting on with?' She pushed the door to shut him out.

The following Monday at three in the morning, Barry and Debbie drove home from the airport wearing sombreros. The kids had fallen asleep in the back, and when they arrived at the bungalow they had to be levered out of the car like two dead bodies. Casey was woken up to pee in case he wet the bed.

'Stay,' Debbie whispered to Barry, shutting Casey's bedroom door quietly. 'It's nice when you stay.'

Something had happened, a tidal change, because now she couldn't get enough of him.

'Their dad,' she'd said by the pool one day, 'I just didn't want to go through that again.'

It was as if a layer had been peeled away. 'I'm not going anywhere,' he said, 'not if you don't want me to.'

He'd had about two hours' sleep when he arrived at the garage later that morning and couldn't understand what was going on. There were papers strewn around the forecourt, the blinds were down on the shop. BACK AT ONE – his dad's baby writing. He left things exactly as they were and drove back into town to the house.

'Dad?' he called as he turned his key in the door. 'Dad, are you there?' He was thinking: *Heart attack. Stroke.*

The downstairs smelt of stale cars. The kitchen was tidy but for a bottle of Coke half-drunk and an empty bottle of Smirnoff. There was a glass in the sink with a fly scrunched up in it; someone had had a cigarette – a dirty brown stub unravelling in the plughole.

'Dad?'

Barry climbed the stairs up to the bedrooms. In his dad's room, lying on the bed, one of those big A3 charity calendars of middle-aged women in their undies. Barry got down on his knees and looked under the bed, straight through to the skirting the other side. He went to the wardrobe. It jangled emptily.

How long had the garage been shut? Why had no one got hold of him?

He drew the curtains and looked down into the yard. It was preternaturally quiet. He stared hard at the shed.

When he got downstairs and out around the back, the air was soft and musty. There was evidence of chickens all around, splotches of bird shit like paint up against the brickwork of the building. Barry went straight over to the shed and twiddled the snib of rotating wood that held the door shut. The wood had warped and was stiff; he pulled the door awkwardly and then, before he could translate what was in there, he lifted his hand to cover his nose and mouth.

It was a battle scene. By the looks of their wattles and combs – torn rubber membrane – they'd been pecking at each other. They must have been locked in for days. Around their eyes were dark purple gashes and rusty spots: three separate bodies, sprawled, touching each other with the forced intimacy disaster brings, around and about them explosions of feather. Barry looked up. There was another one on the perch Stan had made from a curtain pole, roosting, rigid against the back wall. The bird appeared to be looking right at him, an eye that drilled like a nail into his head. *How could you forget!* she seemed to squall, as if he, Barry, were responsible for all the weaknesses of men the world over.

One wing was half-spread towards him, and for a moment he thought she was alive because beneath it, her breast appeared to twitch. He jerked the door further to cast more light and as the structure juddered, she dived head first to the top of the pile of bodies.

There was definitely something in the air. On Sunday afternoon an ambulance had been heard, a stretcher bearing someone from the B & B in the square, Mrs Eastcott's. And Mrs Eastcott had gone away, distraught apparently, to stay with her sister. It was an older man, they thought, someone who'd hung around in the pub, boring them, died in his sleep.

And then Stan. The garage had been closed for over a week and no sign of him. When Barry came back from holiday and reported him missing, Bertram could hardly contain himself. He'd been looking for an excuse to throw in the towel. Said he'd give it until Friday, crossing his fingers.

Friday dawned and still no peep. Although several parents were up in arms about it – the children had put in such a lot of work – Bertram announced that 'sadly' and 'under present circumstances' he felt there was no decent option but to cancel. What if something had happened to Stan – how would they feel then? The money for the dozen or so advance tickets would, of course, be fully reimbursed.

When Sheila turned up nervously that evening in her blue Renault for what she thought was first night, she found herself alone in the community car park. She got out of the car and looked about her as if she were being framed in some way. Her hair was loose and lifted like seed in the evening light. She turned on her heel suddenly, to face the corner of a squat building across the bridge, and then back again to the railings of the bowling green. Something somewhere had moved, scuttling, a mouse or a rat.

Mike had answered the phone when Bertram rang that morning to say the show was off. The Lion, he explained – who, due to cast shortage, was also playing the Wizard – had disappeared. Too much information, Mike groaned.

'Fine, will do,' he said, legs hung over the arm of the sofa.

He'd neglected to pass on the message.

Sheila climbed back into the car. She sometimes used to tot up her marriages on her fingers like Henry VIII, wondering where she would have been if she'd stayed, for instance, with Eustace, or Tony, who'd been rolling in it, selling watches and computers in Bahrain.

A woman on her own's no good, her mother urged her. A husband inspires confidence – don't leave it too long. She could hear the creak of fossil in her bones. Although her mother liked to have pictures to show her friends, Sheila wasn't fooling anyone. She'd let herself go; she'd lost the knack.

It was getting late and it had begun to drizzle. Sheila remained hunched up for over an hour, every now and again wiping a porthole in the condensation to assure herself that there was still nobody out there, until it became too dark to tell the difference.

www.vintage-books.co.uk

ACKNOWLEDGEMENTS

'Richard' and 'Mrs Eastcott' were first published in *Riptide*, Volumes I and II respectively. With thanks to Beaty Rubens who commissioned 'A Taste of Heaven', a version of which was broadcast on Radio 3 in July 2008, and to the Estate of Ted Hughes for kind permission to use the extract from *Moortown Diary* (Faber and Faber, 1989).